# peace
## betrayed

PUNAM FARMAH

Peace Betrayed

A Peace Series Novella



Cover Image and Design: Art Pratt Photography and design

ISBN: **978-1702456913**



The town of Peace, Montana, USA is the intellectual property of author S. H. Pratt. The name and location are graciously allowed to be used in these pages.

Any resemblance to places, persons, and/or events is purely coincidental. No harm is intended.

# dedication:

For Anjna, Nisha and Ketan.
Family

# peace
betrayed

# Chapter 1

"She really doesn't know what she's missing," Melissa's words were cut off with the onset of pure, unadulterated bliss as Devan let his fingers do the talking. Actions had a tendency to speak louder than words.

The rest of him wasn't too far behind. His left hand intertwined with hers amidst the churned-up mess of pale blue sheets that surrounded them. A few moments of rhythm built to a crescendo that kept them both attentive.

"Say nothing," Devan whispered. He trailed his lips from the soft hollow below her right ear, towards a bosom that had been something of a pleasant surprise.

That was where he reveled for a short while; repeatedly at that. Before long, Devan slid aside; he was a spent, sweaty force as he tried to catch his breath. His heart raced, as it enjoyed the climactic peak. Every inch of him was drenched with adrenaline, salt and sweat.

This bed wasn't his. Hell, it didn't belong to Melissa either. Devan wasn't bothered about the bed, not really. As Devan put his hand to his watch on the nightstand, what bothered him was what he was doing in the bed.

Then there was the whole with whom bit too.

According to his watch, it was 3.45 am. He'd been here since yesterday afternoon. Devan had got little or no sleep in between pockets of passion. The passion was strangely liberating. Oakview was ticking over just fine. For the moment, there was no one there waiting for him. The cat was being babysat by the neighbours. Billings was far enough away for no one to interrupt him.

Turning his head, he sighed to focus on the blue-eyed, red head that had lain next to him. Shuffling back into bed, Devan gently placed his hand to her almost porcelain skin. He frowned a little. His rather warm blood was yet to rush back to his brain. Back to where it should have been.

"You do that every time," Melissa opened her eyes to gaze dozily at him. Her lips parted, flashing her pearly white teeth. "You look as though this is the last time; as though this will never happen again. That someone else should do your Hooch Baron books."

Devan inclined his head, his lips twitched. He'd been caught. Perhaps, he'd become predictable. "Only I call you;

we collide," he said, leaning in to steal a kiss. "This happens."

He'd planned to be quick. Only Melissa's fingers had pinched at his thigh to pull him back below the covers. It would be another hour before Melissa surrendered in one last round. She had one hell of an appetite, and Devan could never resist. It was another hour, before Devan would have a power nap. He would need to get home, preferably in one piece and not get pulled over by Deputy Dray. Driving erratically wasn't a good look for the local Hooch Baron.

Devan left Melisa subdued and fast asleep. He had swept aside curly, red locks to land a soft kiss just above her eyebrow. That was what they had agreed. They liked to say hello to one another. Not saying prolonged, painful goodbyes made their reunions that bit more tantalising. Not saying goodbye, kept the door open to the next eventuality.

He'd showered, dressed and even brewed up coffee. Devan sipped it sweet and black as he surveyed the open plan kitchen. A few months ago, on a whim, they had strode into a Realtor. They'd walked out with a fully furnished rental, with a rolling month by month contract. Devan had put down a deposit, signed the paperwork and pocketed two sets of keys. The two sets of keys allowed them to meet in the middle; there was no hanging about long enough to get caught. They could both get in and out, no questions asked.

Devan Coultrie may have been a Hooch Baron, but he was never going to check into a motel. Mr. and Mrs. Smith this wasn't. He had standards, a few principles as well. Licking his lips, he swept away croissant crumbs. Passing his hands through his damp hair, Devan thought about making tracks.

Mr. and Mrs. Smith was for strangers. It was also far more straight-forward.

The drive home was always the same. He would floor the Toyota, crank up the stereo to be surrounded by the thumping bass of soft rock, interspersed with R'n'B. Devan had deliberately created a playlist that helped to patch his soul, begged for absolution and focused on the redemption of lovers who failed to play by the rules. On the journey home, Devan lost himself in how he and Melissa had taken things one step beyond his books. How, Melissa had become far more than just his accountant.

There had been a text message. It had been that simple. His books were a mess; perhaps they could meet. He'd buy lunch. At that point, Devan would have scored null points for seduction. His wife, the love of his life, was lying next to him sound asleep as he'd pressed send.

Raindrops landed onto the windshield, forming splodgy starbursts. A smile crept across his face as wiper blades flicked across the glass. Lunch has been so innocent. So unassuming of what would come next.

Salmon fishcakes, asparagus and new potatoes. Devan remembered his order. He'd refused alcohol as he tapped the side of a crystal-cut tumbler. That was unusual for him. There were plans later with Aditi. Alcohol made for loose lips. Slugging bourbon at lunchtime would have compromised him.

More so, than what would eventually unfold.

Melissa's hand had brushed carelessly against his. They had both been aiming for a bread roll. As with the tumbler, the restaurant was something of a classy joint on the far side of Helena. He'd deliberately looked for somewhere distant; somewhere on the edge of the radar. Somewhere he could rack up expenses that only his accountant would worry about.

Then, Devan had stretched out his long legs; crossing them at the ankle. At six foot, he was gangly at times. His feet had clipped Melissa's. He'd blushed, grinned too.

"I'm sorry," he'd said, glancing below the table. "Of all the people to play footsie with," Devan had glanced up, flexing a brow. For the first time, he noticed the inky blue of her eyes.

"There are far worse things you could do," she had said, biting her lip.

"Oh, really?" he'd enquired, reaching for glass of water. There was some relief in the cold liquid that quenched his lips. Sitting back, his gaze was trained upon her still. He made a silent survey of the woman sat before him. His imagination, and the rest of him, was quietly going into overdrive.

"Playing footsie is nothing," Melissa sat back too, waving her hand dismissively.

Her body language was wonderfully open and inviting. Devan could enter.

If he dared.

"True," he nodded, taking another mouthful of water. He dabbed at his mouth with a mauve napkin. "Melissa," Devan pronounced each syllable delicately. "I'd much rather play with the rest of you. Think of all the things that could happen. You might be my accountant, but I don't think they would be expensed."

There were far better lines that he might have come up with. Only his brain was no longer functioning at an optimum, innocent level. The blood that might have sharpened his focus had gone elsewhere at the speed of light.

The salmon would have to wait. Devan excused himself, he had to make a 'phone call. He'd be in the lobby.

"Give me ten minutes," he had said, rising from his seat. He then collared a waiter, dressed in an impeccable black and white uniform. "Our entrees were delightful," Devan declared, beaming all too unnecessarily. "Could you give us a moment before the main," he added, ham-acting as he patted his stomach.

Devan moved as fast as he could toward the lobby.

Three minutes. Melissa gave him three minutes before she too arrived in the lobby. She'd pretended to look for him. Her acting had been almost as bad as his.

Devan had found an unlocked supply closet. He had loitered, lying in wait. Devan opened the door, wolf-whistled from the shadows and beckoned her in.

Melissa returned to their table first. She'd ordered a steak with chips.

He'd made a pit stop at the rest room, splashed his face with cold water. He'd needed to sober up a little. Devan was yet to meet a mirror that he liked. Tweaking his collar, he smoothed down his crisp, pale blue, buttoned down shirt. Deftly, he tucked the tails back into his navy trousers. Trousers accented by a tan belt, fastened securely to hold back middle-aged spread. He curled his lips into a grimace; his teeth flashing briefly in the harsh light. Looking at his reflection, he noticed how spaced he looked.

"Spaced or empty?" he asked himself.

Mopping his face with a thick, linen towel, he drew in a deep breath. The fabric was balled up, tossed into a wicker basket. Devan rolled down his sleeves, repositioned the cuffs to fasten them. There was no part of this, which was smart. There was no part of this, which was a business transaction.

Rubbing his palms together, he noticed that something was missing. His heart leapt into his mouth. Sat between the hot and cold faucets was his wedding ring. He couldn't walk out of here without it. His conscience kicked in as he picked it up, to thread it back into place. Devan wedged it back on; leaving it behind, really didn't bear thinking about.

Eventually, Devan trundled back. One particular appetite had been satisfied; more than once at that. Not that it had all been fast, frenzied or full of fury. There had also been calm, cool curiosity. His intrigued imagination had been rather mistaken. Devan was hungry when he sat down. Compared to what had he had experienced, eating seemed altogether mundane.

As they ate, there was conversation. They talked about his books, his plans to expand his Hooch Baron Empire.

Hooch Baron.

Devan smiled as he returned back to his car, as he entered Peace. His bubble popped with the bass coming from the stereo.

In his head, Hooch Barons existed only in tawdry paperback novels. They were sort of people who indulged in bodice-ripping. Devan shrugged his shoulders to change the track.

Melissa had giggled the next time that they had met. Apparently, she had walked out of the restaurant with fewer buttons on her blouse and a torn skirt.

He really didn't remember doing that.

Yes, there had been a next time. There was always going to be a next time.

And here he was, months later, going home from yet another rendezvous. There had been no going back from that supply closet.

He was a Hooch Baron.

There had been bodice ripping.

# Chapter 2

There was something wonderfully liberating about plotting world domination in your boxers.

Sat behind his desk, he'd taken a selfie and sent it to his wife. He'd captioned it 'Laundry day'. It was innocent; he was, after all, a gentleman. Glancing at his watch, Devan realised that it had just gone two. He'd been sat there since ten having had a scant breakfast. Scant, but delicious. A mug of tea with some toast. Toast that had been generously spread with raspberry jam.

He'd been sat there working for an NGO, giving advice on investments in Singapore. A few hours graft, had earned him a pretty penny. He wasn't just the local Hooch Baron; he needed to have something of a proper job alongside it all. His stomach continued to growl. Then there was the smell. Devan was also in need of a shower. He'd spent the last two days digging his vegetable patch. He planned to turn some of it over to the ladies who worked with Our Ladies of the Rockies, so they could use the produce for church dinners. Devan had more than enough, sharing it made his soul feel that bit lighter. There were people in this world who had a lot less and every little bit helped.

Closing down his laptop, Devan headed for the shower. He didn't hear the vibration of his 'phone.

In the shower, he rolled his eyes at the fruity shower gel that Aditi liked. Froth and foam washed over his skin; over the infinity tattoo on left pectoral. A souvenir that came from being young and adventurous. Devan had been partying in Amsterdam. He'd paid for it, using money his parents had given him for his birthday. They still didn't know how he'd spent it. He had no plans to tell them.

Once he'd showered, he dressed. He ambled down to the kitchen, found some yellow lentils and got rid of his hunger. Devan settled into being a domestic God, passing a vacuum around the lounge. It was all very agreeable, being a faux house-husband. He wasn't bitter about Aditi bringing home the bacon. It was a fairly straight forward, amiable agreement that they had come to.

When she was here, that was.

Aditi was absent quite a bit.

That was their deal.

Their 'telegraphic marriage'.

He knew there was more to it than that. A someone, rather than a something. Aditi was yet to confess; she was yet to come clean. She was guilty; so was he. Poles apart, the string of their marriage was pulled taut between them. He bored himself with the vacuum, before returning to his study. Devan couldn't be bothered to do any more work. He eyed his desk, the laptop. He noticed his 'phone, it was flashing. Someone wanted his attention.

Heading towards the desk, he prayed it wasn't work. He'd had quite enough of using his brain.

"She trusts you," said the voice on the other end of the line. The voice was raspy, and familiar. "Aditi knows you wouldn't do to her, what she's doing to you. She hasn't got a clue; doesn't think you know. Is it killing you yet? Check your messages. It's definitely not killing her."

Then the line went dead. Christopher Feltham. The man was a complete and utter horse's behind.

Chris hung up with pure defiance. He'd shot a bullet into Devan's brain.

Devan's hands trembled as he checked his messages. Screen shots, messages. Pictures. Aditi. Chris. There was even a video, with a moment of pure ecstasy.

His stomach churned.

As though tainted, the 'phone fell from his hot, sweaty fingers. The device landed with a thud onto his desk.

Running to the bathroom, he nearly fell head-first into the toilet. The contents of his guts made an unsavoury exit.

Later, he called her. Could she get to the apartment, perhaps they could meet? His wife was away, he'd not seen Melissa in a few weeks. He'd bring milk and bread. She'd bring him Bourbon.

The good stuff.

A walk to Brightman's helped to numb some of the pain. He was pulling milk from a refrigerator when he heard his name. Devan must have turned around twice, in a daze, before registering Jay and his daughter.

He waved at Jaycee "Hello, missy, how are you?" Devan couldn't help but coo over the little girl. He couldn't help himself; he did it every time he came across a small child. "You okay there?" a small pudgy hand flexed at him. Jaycee curled her fingers around his.

"She's good," beamed Jay, "Looking for a steak dinner, aren't we?" His face was a picture as Jaycee kissed her father.

"Growing girl, aren't you," Devan laughed as Jaycee grinned. "I can grow you some veg to go with it, just say the word. I'm happy to oblige. Think of all the vitamins and minerals."

"Just no eggplant though," Jay shook his head. "She's not a fan."

"It's eggplant, Jay. Nobody's a fan of eggplant," shrugged Devan. "But noted anyway." He blew raspberries at Jaycee, as she had started to do the same. "Zucchini it is then."

"No Aditi?" Jay looked passed Devan, as though expecting her to show up. "Saw her in Billings, with a colleague. Well, she said he was a colleague. Fellow Brit," his eyes knitted together. "Older, a bit worn around the edges; they looked cosy."

Focused on Jaycee still, Devan could hear the curiosity in Jay's voice. He resisted the urge to let it all out. He'd yet to process it all anyway; it was all too immediate.

"Yeah, a colleague," he stated, "She's starting a legal practice there. Folks fly in from England regularly.

"She did say actually," Jay's attention was regained by Jaycee as she wiggled at this hip. He sounded none too convinced. "There were files and things whilst they ate lunch. You know, we should get going. Don't forget the zucchini."

Devan watched Jay and his little girl carry on shopping. Colleague. He knew that bit wasn't true. Paying for the milk, Devan headed to Billings at full throttle.

She had brought him over. Here, to Montana, and so close to Peace.

His Peace was now a shattered Peace. Devan could feel every fracture, every fissure that had formed.

This town really wasn't big enough for the two of them.

Devan didn't use his keys at the apartment. He rang the doorbell; he'd seen her car out front. Devan attacked the doorbell savagely; bile and anger rose within him. The door swung open; he heard his name. Milk and bread cascaded from his grip. Kicking the door closed, he swept Melissa into his arms. He was all fingers and thumbs as he removed a midnight blue negligee and kissed skin that looked almost luminescent. Skin that looked almost good enough to eat.

He made no apologies to lift her up, edge to the bedroom and slam a second door. Fury and frisson combined. He would apologise later for having thrown her onto the bed and with some force.

Devan Coultrie was a man possessed. He was hot-blooded and in dire need of release.

At that moment in time, he said nothing. Words really wouldn't cut it.

□

# Chapter 3

He sulked for days. Having received the call from Chris, Devan had viewed the pictures over and over. Eventually, he deleted them. His sulk had led him to cleaning the house from top to bottom. Then there had been 'phone calls.

'Phone calls to Melissa.

"You in a pickle there, Devan?" she'd asked, giggling across the line. "Can't be your balance sheet; I've checked that already. The problem must lie in your bedsheets. Are they a bit cold and empty?"

"Something like that," he'd replied. "I'm going slightly crazy, not having anyone to play with."

"Oh really?" Melissa had taken a breath, to purr across the line. "How could I help, Mr. Coultrie?"

"Don't," Devan had laughed wickedly. "Mr.Coultrie is my father. You and I don't have that's sort of relationship."

"Amen to that," she'd giggled, sending a wave down his spine. "Is it my voice that you wanted to hear, or did you want to get a hold of me instead?"

Both options had bloomed in his head, his imagination had wandered. Devan knew every inch of Melissa with his eyes closed. His fingertips had explored everything and then some; there was no part of her that he couldn't map.

"Both," he replied. His heart had raced as his imagination had moved through the motions.

"Do you miss her?" Melissa had asked the one question that was perpetually strung between them. "Do you miss your wife?"

"With every breath," Devan didn't need to be asked twice. "Aditi; that's her name. No need to take it. You're not her."

"She hurt you," Melissa lost brownie points for stating the obvious.

"And I'm doing the same," he had spat the words outs. "There are no excuses for doing what I'm doing."

"Yet, *you* called *me*." There was hurt, some disdain too, in her voice. "Still we go around in circles."

"I know," He'd been cleaning the stairs, a yellow cloth was draped over the bannister. "Melissa. I'm sorry." Biting his lip, he hung up. Devan sat on the stairs a while, thinking about all things domestic. Had he vacuumed everywhere, did the bathroom need scrubbing? He couldn't remember the last time that he'd taken down the drapes to give them a good clean.

If there had been silverware that would have featured. Devan felt alone, listless and very lost. His home was empty, as was his heart. In dire need of a distraction, he headed to the kitchen. There was only one thing for it.

He was going to clean the oven.

Finding the necessary kit, he plugged his 'phone into a dock. An apron was pulled on, tied at his waist. Devan selected a playlist, opened the oven and got on with it.

With his head in the oven, the music playing; he didn't register the sound of his name. He didn't hear the jangle of keys, the sound of stilettos travelling across the floor. So when his backside was goosed, Devan screamed blue murder to jump out of his skin. His heart thumped hard as he turned around to land into Aditi's arms.

"Hello, gorgeous," she grinned vapidly. Before long, his face was smothered in cranberry-coloured lipstick.

Wrapping his arms around her waist, Devan let her plunder at will.

"Missed me?" she gasped, as he ventured halfway down her neck.

"Just a bit," he'd been barely able to breathe, never mind speak.

"Show me," Aditi whispered, her fingers had already made short work of his fly.

Using one hand to unbutton her jeans, Devan bundled his wife into his arms; he headed towards the breakfast bar.

"Tell me you love me," his words were strained, he really couldn't breathe. "That you'd never hurt me." Pinning Aditi in place, he threw away a chair.

"I do, I love you," Aditi pulled him closer, as Devan towered over her.

Every inch of Aditi vibrated against him. Placing a finger to her lips, he tugged her legs around his waist. He didn't need to hear any more. Reunion and reconciliation were all too good but didn't last long. At half passed midnight, he clambered into bed, exhausted. He'd left Aditi downstairs, plugged into her laptop. Dressed only in a pair of polka-dotted boxers, he slid into crisp, clean, cold sheets. He would forgive her this, him going to bed alone. She'd come home and there'd be a connection. Devan fell asleep; he was exhausted but had thoroughly enjoyed himself. Now to dream and enjoy that too.

His '63 Lincoln moved effortlessly down the drive, to arrive outside of the house. He glanced out of the window to smile at the ochre oaks that surrounded the house as autumn kicked in. Parking up, he noted the apple pie cooling on the windowsill. A smile formed behind the cigarette that billowed at his lips. Taking one last drag, he tossed aside the butt as he clambered out. Out came his hat, a valise from the backseat. The scent of apple pie welcomed him at the door.

"Honey, I'm home," Devan declared. His hat landed on the coat stand, his bag was planted near a bucket of umbrellas. Born and raised in Britain, there were always going to be umbrellas in the house.

"So you are," Aditi appeared in the lounge. Her hair was pulled into a neat bun; her eyes were lined with kohl. Her ruby red lips rather made his knees go weak. Dressed in a powder blue sari, her curves and contours were accentuated enough to happily engage his imagination. Slowly, seductively, she glided across the floor toward him.

"I made pie," she twittered, tracing a finger across his cheek. "There's a pot roast for dinner, lots of fluffy, roasted potatoes.

"Divine," sighed Devan, stealing the ruby from her red lips. "All smells good enough to eat."

Aditi's hand slid into his breast pocket, to find a carton of cigarettes. She nudged one out, before reaching into his back pocket for his lighter. Aditi planted the cigarette between her lips. Taking another, she nudged against his teeth.

"Not good for you, apparently," Devan watched as Aditi lit both cigarettes. As she'd tucked one between his lips; he'd been poised to kiss her.

"Neither's butter," she said, taking a drag and hold the cigarette between her painted fingers. "All good things and in moderation. Drink?"

"Oh, yes," he replied, watching her as she floated away. He loosened his red, silk tie. It was one of his favourites. It was a gift from Aditi when he had first started at the beer company. He was the head of Acquisitions and rather liked the gig. The job came with interesting perks, one of which happened to be his secretary. She had the most delightful red hair. The thought whirled around his head as Aditi handed him a glass of bourbon.

"Drink that, rest up," she said, beaming. "Wash up though. I'll give you a call when dinner's done."

He was transfixed as she waltzed away. Devan savoured the wiggle. It was always the same; she could be in a sari today, twin-set and pearls tomorrow. She was all his. He was one lucky man and then some. Dinner was a delight, he ate heartily. Devan listened to Aditi regale him about the plans for Founder's Day. There was something about a bake sale and how she was going to part of a sewing bee. He hung on her every word. He was, however, distracted. But kept things quiet.

All he could think about was his secretary. The way she walked, the turn of her ankles; the way she said his name.

"Mr. Coultrie, would you like sugar in your tea?"

That was her greeting the next morning. He was always prompt, getting to his desk for a quarter to eight.

She asked him that every morning.

"Two, Miss. Bainbridge," he replied. "Just a moment though," he'd said looking up from the black and white photo on his desk. "Close the blinds for me," Devan nodded, pushing his chair back a little.

"Of course," Miss. Bainbridge smiled delicately, tucking a stray strand of her hair behind her ear. Her hair was coiled away into a chignon, accentuating the curve of her neck.

Devan watched the movement of her hips as she moved. His eyes wandered down her hem, down towards her feet. He knew exactly what lay above the hemline. Learning the ropes at the beer company, had been more than looking at fixed assets. There were stockings, suspenders and always a garter belt.

"If you have a moment," he smirked as Melissa twirled the string of pearls around her neck. They always nestled neatly against her bosom.

"Would you like me to take down a dictation?" she asked, her eyes glimmered.

Devan Coultrie wouldn't make her ask twice. He never had to.

Something jolted him awake, made him reach out. His hands landed against the curve of Aditi's spine. She muttered something in the sleep. He didn't quite make it out. At least she had found her way to their bed. Sliding across, he curled his limbs around her. She turned over, her arms and legs snaking across his form.

It had been a dream. Nothing more, nothing less.

□

# Chapter 4

It would take the best part of a week for Devan's sleep to settle. He'd spend that week, sleeping anchored in Aditi's arms. Aditi was in his hearth and home; that was where he wanted her. That was where she belonged. She didn't have to go anywhere. Devan prized it all; it all felt perfect, much like a dream. So when he was prodded awake one Saturday morning, he might as well have landed in another universe.

"Devan, you awake?" Aditi poked him in the ribs, the stomach; it was strangely comforting.

Bleary eyed, Devan sat up, uncurling his legs. There was a pot of tea, a full English breakfast on a tea-tray balanced on the bed with its legs either side of his. He was all very confused as he pulled the tray close.

"You've cooked all week, I wanted to say thank you," Aditi slid closer a little, to kiss his cheek. "Breakfast in bed, for the man I love. For the man, who loves me."

Still he said nothing, but rubbed his stubble-clad jaw.

"And there's more," she said sidling in alongside. "I popped into Brightman's yesterday. Thought we could go have a picnic in the park, perhaps."

Tucking into the breakfast, Devan groaned in pure pleasure. She'd hit the mother lode with herbed sausages.

"We could go to McBride Memorial," said Aditi, curling an arm around his. "Lounge. Do nothing. Spend quality time together. Plus, it's your birthday soon…."

And there it was. There was a kicker.

"You won't be around," he chewed on bacon to gulp it down. Aditi's fingers had made it to his hand and fiddled with this wedding band.

"You've lost weight," she commented. "Don't tell your mum. She'll worry, tell the Grannies. They'll tell me I'm neglecting you. Look, every minute that I spend with you. It's pure, it means the world to me. I spend so much time away from you, it makes my heart hurt."

As he pulled a fork out his mouth, Devan felt his wedding ring fall off.

"Hey!" the fork clattered to his place. Devan pulled his hand back as his wedding ring flew into the air. He held out his palm to catch it.

Aditi had recoiled back. "What?" she asked, blinking furiously.

"Don't do that," he grumbled, threading the band back on. "That doesn't move; it doesn't come off. Even if I cease to exist, you cremate me with it. Don't ever take it off again." Anger flashed across his face. He took a few moments, centered himself with his breakfast. "A picnic, the memorial park?"

Aditi nodded. She looked a little as though she had been scalded. He also saw fear; he'd never seen that before.

"Fine," he said, scooping up breakfast. "Quality time."

Hurtling toward his right hand was a bright pink, luminous Frisbee. Stretching out his frame, Devan was almost diagonal to catch it. He was most certainly horizontal as he landed to catch it. He and Aditi had spent most of the day at the McBride Memorial Park. He'd been sprawled out on the picnic blanket whilst in Aditi's arms as they'd enjoyed their picnic.

"How drunk are you?" he asked Aditi as she ran into him. "Your aim is atrocious."

Aditi picked blades of grass from his shirt. "What can I say, you're wonderfully disorientating?" she grinned, before pulling him into her arms. "Can't blame the bourbon and cola. It's nice out here," she commented, threading her fingers into his back pockets.

"Isn't it just," he let out a contented sigh. "I must admit, this is one of your better ideas." They shifted on the spot to see Jay Terry, walking with his wife and daughter.

"Oh, she is cute," Aditi cooed.

"We could have one," Devan felt equally dreamy. "We've let things slide a bit, but we could have one of those." He watched the little girl toddle around as her parents watched her every move.

"Things have gone awry, yeah" nodded Aditi. "You're broody, sad too. I can hear it in your voice. We could have one of those; we should get things back on track.

"Seriously?" he ventured, somewhat fearful.

"Seriously," came the reply. "The place in Billings is nearly done. I won't be gone as much. I can be here more, with you. No real reason not to, Devan. I'm ready when you are."

"I am," he drew her close, inhaling her scent. "Ready and waiting."

As the sun set, they tidied away their banquet.

"We should do this more often," Devan commented, bundling up a wicker basket as they made their way home. "This was lovely. Me, you; lots of quality time. This was pure bliss, Ms.Rao."

"We can," Aditi kissed his cheek, to take his hand. "We will. We can lovely, whenever you want."

In a couple of days, she would be gone, and this would make both Devan's heart and head hurt.

In a couple of days, it was Devan's birthday.

"Devan Coultrie?"

"Yeah?" Devan yawned, having answered the front door. He was up stupidly early, and dressed in his pyjamas.

"Delivery for you," said the courier; a fair-haired adolescent with grey eyes. He handed Devan a white, cardboard box.

"Great. What is it?" asked Devan, bleary eyed and blind as a bat.

"Cake," said the teen, jabbing a finger at the lid. The name of a bakery in Billings was embossed the top. "Enjoy, and have nice day."

"Cake," muttered Devan. "What the flip do I need cake for?"

"Your birthday," replied Aditi, she fiddled with an earring as she came down the stairs. At the bottom was a set of cases. She was ready to leave. "You have an appointment later, at Toppins," she spoke as she curled her hair in a ponytail. "I had a word with Mike. Take the cake. Jericho, Clancy and Jay will meet you there about eight. You have food, drink. Kyle might show too."

Standing there, his mouth fell agape as he held onto the cake box. There was one last kiss and a cuddle before Aditi left.

A boozy party at Toppins. She wasn't entirely useless.

Devan was more than punctual. He was early, as he arrived at Toppins clutching at the cake box.

"Get in here," Mike waved at him, as Devan loitered at the door. "We know who you are, where you live too. No need to look so worried." Mike beckoned Devan toward the bar.

"I know nothing," declared Devan as he warily put the box on the bar. "What did she do, what did Aditi say to you?"

"That it's your birthday," replied Mike. He opened the box, to delicately remove the cake. "That hell would freeze over, before you spend two days sulking at Oakview. Go sit, the boys will be here soon. She's a good woman. Throwing you a booze and bar party." Setting aside the cake, Mike poured Devan a beer. "She's got a five-hundred-dollar bar bill, and then I send you home. The taxis are included too actually, for all of you."

Devan took his beer, settled into a booth and waited. Bang on eight, the boys arrived.

"You don't look a day over fifty," Jericho arrived first, landing a broad hand to Devan's shoulder.

"The man is pickled," Clancy declared, tipping his hat. "The Peace Hooch Baron drinks too much of his own stash."

"And refuses to ride in rodeos," Jay swept into the bar too. The party of four settled themselves into a corner, the booth was safe with no room to be sorry. There was drinking, eating; a fair bit of cake was consumed too.

"This is probably the first ever, bloke-booze-birthday cake party to ever happen here," Devan was only just sitting up right. He'd drunk a fair bit already; too quick and too soon.

"Aditi done well," slurred Jericho, raising his glass.

"Fed us, helped us get drunk," Clancy rubbed his stomach contentedly.

"Good wholesome fun," laughed Jay. There were glasses clinking all over. "Better than sulking whilst home alone."

"I don't sulk," protested Devan, slurring. "My own company is great; just great, thanks."

"Ours is better," trilled Clancy, slinging back a shot. "Misery loves company."

"And beer. Oh, excuse me," Jay had suddenly gone a funny shade of green. He squeaked, to make a retreat to the rest room.

"Devan Coultrie, there you are!" The Scottish-American twang of Kyle McCoy cut across the bar.

Devan tried to get up but couldn't muster it. "All here indeed," he really wasn't at optimum capacity. "Aditi tell you?"

"Easy there," Kyle laughed as a chair was pulled up. "She did. I got a bit delayed but made it. Oh, there's cake."

Finding it difficult, Devan surveyed the gang sat before him. He was well and truly toasted.

They ate, they drank. They didn't break anything or start a fight. They were all very civilised in making short work of Aditi's bar bill. At the end of the evening, Devan looked at Mike behind the bar. He didn't need to say anything. Before long, the taxis came. They all went home, wobbling out of the bar, singing and laughing.

Even the local Hooch Baron had to draw the line somewhere.

He'd enjoyed his appointment at Toppins. Devan appreciated the fact that Aditi had taken the time, made the effort to organise it all. There was still celebrating to be done though; his actual birthday was until the next day. Despite the ribbing about being home alone and in a sulk, that was exactly what he planned to do.

Devan surfaced at about half eleven the next morning. Slowly but surely, he made his way downstairs to the kitchen. Slowly and surely, was the order of the day. As daylight streamed in, life unfolded; it was all too loud and too bright.

It took him twenty minutes to make tea. It would've been simple; to boil the kettle, throw a teabag in to a mug. No, this had to be done the hard way. A saucepan sat on the stove, with hot water, spices and a couple of teabags thrown in.

That wasn't just tea. That was rocket fuel.

In twenty minutes, the spices would infuse with the tea bags. It would also take twenty minutes for the clock strike twelve. At that point, Devan could legitimately dose his tea with bourbon.

Bourbon and on his birthday. Felt like a good idea.

Gingerly, he went to fridge. Devan found the milk and splashed it into the saucepan. Twice, during the night, he had woken to hug the toilet. Most of the booze and bar food had exited. He felt more than fragile at that moment in time.

Opening and closing cupboards, he tried to find a teapot. He felt as though he needed to drink his Birthday Bourbon from a teapot. Eventually, he found one and was about to fill it. However, it almost dropped it as the letterbox rattled. To this day, he had yet to install a mailbox.

"Don't have picket fence," Devan muttered. "Don't need a flipping mailbox." Pulling his robe closed, he tied it with the cord. He shuffled out of the kitchen, to his front door. A heap of mail was sat upon the mat.

"Bill, Bill," he shuffled through the stack. Then Devan recognised his sister's handwriting, and almost keeled over. She'd sent a card. He opened it up; there was an old, wrinkly man on the front. Inside, Aida, Rohan and Libby had signed it. Taped opposite was a crisp ten-pound note and a pound coin. How he missed the Pound Sterling.

"Mum sent you the money," he read. "Don't you dare spend it all in Toppins. Mike will tell us." Devan actually laughed out aloud; his head throbbed. As he turned the card over, he saw one of his baby pictures. He was a pink-faced bundle, all tightly swaddled in his mother's arms. Below the image was his full name and his birth weight.

Devan Raaj Coultrie. Seven pounds and four ounces.

The kitchen clock struck twelve. Devan took one look at the tea. Satisfied that it had brewed enough, he decanted a third into a tea pot. Deciding against the bourbon, he put the teapot onto a tray with some sugar and a mug. He would sit on the sofa, do nothing.

All was quiet. All was serene. He was alone, but he was far from miserable.

Devan definitely wasn't sulking.

Setting down the tray, he grabbed the remote to turn on the T.V. He turned the volume down a little, to watch the pretty pictures without his brain combusting. He was about to lose himself in something sugary and mundane. Only for the doorbell to ring; his letterbox rattled again and there were voices.

Devan sat there for a moment, convinced that he was hallucinating.

"DEVAN COULTRIE!!"

That would be him.

"Open up, man," that one was Gaelic sounding; he knew that hum.

He bolted to the door, letting it swing open.

"What took you so long?" in stepped Kyle, wearing sunglasses.

"Coultrie, good afternoon," Next came Jericho, tipping his hat.

"Sshhhhh," Clancy pressed a finger to his lips. "Not so loud. Jeez…where's your coffee?"

"Jay?" Devan rubbed both eyes, as Jay stepped in carrying bags from Brightman's.

"The one and only," he replied, closing the door behind him and ushering Devan back into the lounge.

Looking at each one in turn, Devan absorbed the scene before him. Clancy, was absent as he rattled around the kitchen. He could hear him rummage cupboards all too noisily. Then there was the singing; the singing was a bit much.

"Chai, good thinking," Jericho had poured a mugful to raise it in salute.

Kyle sat in an armchair, his head thrown back. "This hangover," he said, all very pained. "Isn't my fault. This, I blame Aditi for. She paid for one hell of a drinking session."

"And this too," Jay unpacked the bags onto the coffee table. "Ribs, wings, fries and slaw. Ready to throw into your kitchen." He looked back up at Devan with a grin. "Happy Birthday."

"What's going on?" Devan rubbed his stomach. The mere sight of food was frightening.

"A hangover rescue," said Jericho, blowing into his tea. "For the day after the night before. Plus," he said, dropping sugar into his mug. "No sulking, no misery. Your wife left detailed instructions. We're just following them."

"Woah, hold that thought," Jay waggled a finger, before rooting around in the bags.

Shaking his head, Devan threw his hands into the air. Clancy walked into the room with a second tray. The scent of coffee collided with that of Chai. He had mugs. A cafetière too.

"Hair of the dog," Kyle half laughed as he eyed the bottle of bourbon that Jay had pulled out. He set to helping Clancy with the coffee.

"Tea for me," Devan quickly interjected. "For now, that is."

Jay laughed to grab a coffee from Kyle. "Oh, we have time," he said with a sigh. "And a very big bottle."

Devan picked up a tea, and raised it. For the life of him, he couldn't think of a toast.

"To Aditi Rao!" declared Kyle. "And one of hell of hangover."

Aditi's name rang out around the room. With a shrug, Devan joined in. There was no sulking, no misery. For the moment, he wasn't alone.

□

# Chapter 5

Today he would have to bite his tongue, watch his mouth and keep his mind clean. All he had to do was keep a lid on pain and fury.

"Remember to breathe," said Aditi, her words crackled over the line as he closed the 'fridge. "They are older, of a different generation and from two different cultures. For two old ladies, this is one hell of an adventure."

"I know," Devan couldn't help but let out a pained sigh. He poured milk onto his cereal. "That's what worries me; that they get here safely. Then I can deal with whatever they throw at me."

"Throw at us *both*, Devan," Aditi tutted sharply. "I'll be home for dinner," she added. "Once I've finished with the contractors. Oh, and Devan?"

"Yeah?" he was intrigued, as he shoveled cereal into his mouth. Even after everything, the way she spoke his name brought him to his knees.

"Don't mention the crockery," she said; her tone rather grave. "Seriously."

He chuckled quietly. He knew exactly what happened to a piece of Granny Gloria's Wedding China. That had made Thanksgiving a little more interesting.

"We'll see," he commented lightly. "You know my Grannies. They both have ways of making me behave."

"As do I," Aditi laughed. "But that's how we ended up with damaged goods. Okay, fine. Have fun. I'll see you. Love you."

"You to," he replied, hanging up. "I shouldn't," he told himself. "But I don't think I can stop." He ate his cereal, keeping an eye on the clock. It had just gone eleven. His Grannies, who had travelled together, would land just after one. He was already a little behind. Aditi had waylaid him this morning, before heading to work. He had been taken, quite literally, by surprise. He took her when he could; she was doing the same. Devan had no grounds to complain.

He made a mental note to strip their bed as he drank tea. Clean sheets might help him keep a clean mind.

Between Aditi and Melissa, there were all sorts of unsavoury things going through his head.

Melissa. His blue-eyed, red-haired beauty.

He drank his tea, dropping his mug into the sink as her face bloomed across his mind.

Devan had a decision to make. He wondered if he wanted forgiveness or absolution. He'd need Father Stephen for that. Confession was after all, good for the soul. Not that Aditi had confessed. If she wasn't worried about her soul, perhaps he didn't need to worry about his.

By half two-he left time for immigration-Devan was present and correct in arrivals at the airport. Passing a palm through his hair, he glanced at the hair band on his wrist. He'd pinched it off Aditi and quite forgotten about it. Neither one of his Grannies, liked his hair.

It was another fifteen minutes before the special assistance cart rolled up. He heard his Grannies, before he saw them.

"Ah, there he is!" exclaimed the one. "Devan, over here! Oh, he needs a haircut. Such long hair, like a girl."

"Yes, over there, that way," trilled the second. "Oh, I know. Why does he wear it so long? Richard was the same," Gloria commented. "He's going bald now, so I don't need to worry. Did he see us yet?"

The cart sped up to get closer.

"Devan!" yelled Daya, waving at him. Yellow, gold bangles jangled at her wrists.

"Hello!" he exclaimed, making his way to them as the cart came to a stop. For a moment, Devan was confused. He had no idea which granny to hug first. He watched as they helped each other of the cart, before hurtling toward him.

"Big hug!" Gloria beamed. "You take one side, Daya."

"And you take the other," Daya pinched his cheeks. He was quickly engulfed by the pair of them.

"You're a bit thin," Gloria had found his stomach and patted at it.

"Aditi not feeding you?" Daya rubbed his chees with a tissue. "Maybe we need to speak with her, about being a good wife. Where is she?"

Devan felt his face flush, his stomach flipped.

"Oh, no, that's okay," he stuttered a little. "She's feeding me just fine," Devan tried to smile. "Besides, I know my kitchen better than she does. She's at work, will be home later. Let's get you pair to Oakview."

The two Grannies looked at one another; neither looked convinced.

"She's not here, he's not well fed," Daya eyed him. "She's always away."

"You worry too much," Gloria took Daya by the arm. "This is America, they're youngsters. They live in a Brave New World. Here, my sweet, we are the dinosaurs."

Devan let it all slide. He was happy that they were here, that they had landed safely.

"You two are very special," he said, there was a granny either side of him. "I love you more than I will ever be able to say."

Daya gave him a wary, side-ways glance. "You about to cry, Devan?" she asked, all very concerned.

"He might," offered Gloria. "Get us home, Devan. We're old, tired and need to rest."

It didn't take long, but they got into Devan's Toyota and en route to Oakview. No sooner were the two Grannies buckled up, they both fell asleep in the back.

Devan got them home. Each granny was ensconced in her respective room. As they settled in, he prepared afternoon tea. Bang on four, he called up the stairs.

"Grannies," he'd yelled. "It's time for tea and in the walled garden."

He wandered off to make sure everything was just right for them. He passed through the kitchen to pick up two vintage cake stands that Aditi had found in Colorado. He'd set the table with Granny Gloria's china, just to make things special. In the walled garden, he set the cake stands down. He sat and waited for the Grannies to make their way down. It was fifteen minutes before they appeared.

"This looks lovely," Gloria beamed, her hands clasped together as she surveyed the afternoon tea. There was cake, sandwiches. Teapots with cosys too. "All this cake, Devan. You'll trigger my diabetes."

"Life's too short," retorted Daya, pulling out a chair. "My tea cosy," she tugged at the one, Daya had knitted it, and sent it over via special delivery. The two women cooed over the food as they stacked their plates.

"I'd forgotten how house-trained you are," Gloria chirruped as she poured tea. The she nibbled at a sandwich. "You do make a good one of these."

"Still can't make chappatis though," Daya raised a brow at him. "Give him a bag of lentils…those aren't too bad, actually."

"Better than Aditi's," replied Devan, pouring his own tea. "Compared to her, I'm a gold standard Gourmet."

Then he caught the glance that his grandmothers exchanged.

"Why is she never here?" posed Daya, lifting her teacup with both hands. "Aditi spends all her time flying around, more than…."

"Perhaps she's still not settled," offered Gloria. "She works here, there and everywhere."

"No, she shouldn't," Daya was no longer being polite. "She should be here, and with him!" she flicked a finger toward him.

"What did you do?" Gloria was direct. "After all this time, after everything, did you scare the girl away? Trust you to be a married man, acting like a bachelor."

"What, me?" Devan blinked, dazed at being ambushed. "Why would *I* do anything?" he all but squeaked. "*I* did the right thing. Married the woman I love, trying to set up home and hearth here, Grannies."

"Didn't invite us though," grumbled Daya, going to work on a piece of sponge cake. "That's a separate issue. You should be together, the pair of you."

"It's complicated," he declared, blowing across his tea. "I'm here, I'm not going anywhere. This is home for both of us. Aditi will come home to roost, she always does. Eat up, Grannies, it's all getting cold."

Sipping his tea, Devan hoped that would keep them quiet. They didn't need to know how Aditi had betrayed him.

"Aditi, I like," said Daya. "I can understand her; she's been good to me. Carly," she shook her head a moment. "Was never my cup of tea."

"Always so distant," Gloria nodded as she spoke. "As though she had somewhere else to be, somewhere better. As though, we weren't good enough. The way she used to push and pull you. Can't say I liked her, either. She never visited me, for one. Aditi does. Carly, well, she never gave me the time of day."

"Agreed," Daya clinked her cup against Gloria's. "You're right; you're absolutely right."

"Aditi's not perfect," Devan fiddled with a muffin case. "I'm not saying Carly was. I refuse to speak ill of the dead, Grannies."

"Going to speak ill of Aditi?" Daya squinted in his direction. "It's complicated, my left foot. Don't lie to us, boy."

Once more, the two Grannies eyeballed each other. They were a rather dynamic tag team.

"She doesn't clean up after herself," Devan knew he was squirming. This was altogether uncomfortable. "I'm her husband, not the cleaner. Aditi will quite happily make a mess of everything. Sorting things out, coming clean; not really her forte."

Both Grannies groaned to sit back and retreat. Technically, he'd told the truth.

In something of a sulk, Devan was quiet as tea continued. Gloria and Daya talked between themselves and enjoyed the spread. After which, they both retired for a nap. It was dinner time, before they both arose.

Only there was a catch.

"Fine, I'll tell them," Devan huffed as he hung up his 'phone. Standing in his kitchen, he then launched the device across the worktop.

"Everything okay?" Daya asked, she was stood by the sink washing zucchini.

"Aditi?" Gloria was bang on the money as she chopped peppers.

"She's not coming," Devan muttered, putting his hands to a couple of brown onions. "We can still have dinner without her. Not that she liked Ratatouille anyway."

Once again, Daya and Gloria exchanged looks. Devan bit his tongue. Stuck with clients. He didn't believe that for a minute.

# Chapter 6

The Grannies stayed for nine days. Devan suspended all things Hooch Baron to spend quality time with them. Aditi had flitted in and out: she'd spent a couple of afternoons with them. He'd been surprised on two counts. Firstly, as it was quality family time and completely uninterrupted. Secondly, the two Grannies had poked and prodded her about being such an absent wife. Aditi had taken it in her stride, telling them how she was setting up her practice in Billings. In the long run, she planned to be at home. She and Devan would spend more time together, they were even thinking about starting a family.

The last part had stopped his Grannies in their tracks. Devan was inclined to believe Aditi's plans, when he saw them happen.

The Grannies even made a visit to the Brewer's Barn before they left.

"I don't' understand this at all," Wrinkling up her nose, Daya made feelings quite plain. Sitting at the long table that ran the length of building, she shook her head in disgust. "You carry on, Gloria," she added, pushing up her glasses.

"Don't mind if I do," Gloria walked along one wall, counting the demi-johns of fruit-infused liqueurs and spirits. "Oh, any of this ready?" she asked, tapping the one labelled 'Raspberry Gin.'

"One step ahead," Devan headed towards some shelves, to retrieve a bottle wrapped in brown paper. At the table, he unscrewed the lid to pour a couple of shots.

They were there a while. There was even a shot contest.

Six hours later, Gloria had sobered up. She didn't believe in slugging gin slowly; rum, either. She and Daya boarded their flight back to the North of England. They would visit Rohan, Libby and the Bump before heading back to Middle England.

Devan drove home afterwards, smiling as he remembered the memories made. He'd taken both Grannies to Our Lady of The Rockies, and they'd cooed over Father Stephen. The rest of Peace had also met with them. The diner had been a favourite. Granny Daya had enjoyed her pancakes, and Devan's too. When he returned home the sun had set, the moon was rising. Aditi was away, having flown to London. He warmed up some green lentils, to spend the evening before the television. With an empty house, Devan felt the heavy weight of solitude as it hung in the air.

Once he'd eaten, he picked up his 'phone to check in with his brother.

"Good morning, fella," came the reply on connection. "This early in the day, I do hope you've won the lottery or something." Rohan yawned across the line. "It's Devan, his number flashed."

He had to laugh, if only quietly.

"Thought I'd call," he said, rubbing his eyes. "Tell you that the Grannies are en route. They left here safe and sound."

"They survived Peace, Montana, then, eh?" There was whimsy in Rohan's voice; it didn't appear often. "Great, Libby and I will pick them up later. No doubt we'll get the full match report on you and Aditi. Did you get another baby talk? Gloria's okay. Nani Daya presses the buttons. Hold on, I'll stick you on loudspeaker. Libby's throwing me evils."

"She was all right, actually," Devan replied. "They both were. They were more interested in interrogating Aditi. Weren't too happy about the whole telegraphic marriage thing."

"No-one is happy about that," Stated Libby. "Six months gone, Devan. If it's not the bump driving me nuts, it's hearing you pine and mope. Does that woman ever stop at home with you?"

"Libby," Devan heard Rohan mutter in the background. "You sound like the Grannies. It's complicated."

"No, it's not," Rohan dived straight in. "It's weird. One of you needs to lay down the law. Aditi should decide. What will you do, if you have babies? Try that with a telegraphic marriage. If this was one of those lame-ass novels, I'd put twenty pence on one of you playing away."

"Well, you've made twenty pence," replied Devan, too quick to bite his tongue.

The line pulled taut between them, vibrating with curiosity.

"Why you paying him, Devan?" Libby slashed the silence. "Who the flip is playing away? My God, I will brain you two."

"Wait, hold on, calm," Rohan's breath crackled across the line. "If you get antsy, the bump gets antsy. He's probably taking the-Devan, you taking the rise? Sending my wife's blood pressure sky-high isn't funny."

He took one centering breath.

"Aditi is cheating on me," he gulped to let loose the sentence. "Thing is, she has no idea that I know. This has yet to come out in the wash. I need you pair to keep it that way. No telling Aida yet, either. I'm begging you."

Passing his tongue over his lips, Devan used his palms to sweep away tears that sat in the hollows of his eyes.

"Deal with him," Rohan coughed, "I can't talk to him. He's an idiot. This is stupid."

"Ro-" Devan knew he was gone. "Libby, you there?" Hearing beeps, he figured he was off loudspeaker.

"You're not lying are you," posed Libby, sounding confused. "What happened, you were both so happy."

"Things changed," he replied, sniffing into a sleeve. "No idea when or why it all went pear-shaped. It did, and that's the way things are; pear-shaped." Half of that was a lie.

Libby sounded breathless across the line. "Sorry," she said, "Bump squashing my ribs. Who, what…."

"Chris," Devan just about said the name. "The Ex, he told me. Called, it was a video call. She was in his bed. It's a mess. Then, I…."

He had to get it out.

"Lib, I might have done something stupid too." Devan bit his lip. "It's not revenge, retaliation or rebuttal. I can't give it a name, it's not an excuse."

"Devan, Sweetie…." Libby whispered his name.

"Once I knew, I couldn't not know," he sobbed, sniffed and brushed away tears that fell freely. "So I did the same. I've cheated on her too. We've betrayed each other. She broke her vows, I broke mine."

Libby continued to listen.

"It'll stop," he said firmly, coughing away phlegm. "I can't carry on doing this to myself."

"Is she local?" Libby asked; her tone was wary. "Crapping in your own backyard, Coultrie, is never a good idea."

"Yes and no," Devan snorted to get rid of bogeys.

"Is she, is Aditi, you know, still…" Libby let out a weary breath.

"Yes, I think so," he could feel his heart race Then there was a horrible wave of nausea that passed over him. "I'm starting to go a little mad. I don't know what's worse. I switch between angry, hurt or being just as stupid. I've been just as reckless, vindictive too. I could've been the bigger, better man."

"You still could be," Libby was doing her best to be supportive. She was listening, when he had expected her to give up. "End it, with the other one. Sulk, hurt, flipping well get angry. Just don't hurt yourself, Devan. After everything, all that you've been through. Retreating to Peace, for one. It was all so picture perfect; a postcard. Don't let this become a shattered peace.

"Will you tell Rohan, put him in the picture…." He didn't want to think about the potential response.

"I'll see," Libby replied. "He's a bit peeved right now. Not just because of you. I toss and turn most nights. He spent a few nights on the sofa. I've only just pulled him back into the bedroom. Do the right thing, Devan. Look after yourself. I know what you'll do with bourbon. That, my sweet, never ends well. Don't drown yourself at the bottom of a bottle. I need to go. Rohan's making noises in the kitchen. He always manages to break something." Hanging up, Libby left him to his own devices.

Devan looked at his keys. Drowning himself in a bottle didn't sound too bad, all things considered. He'd walk; he'd only end up giving his keys to Mike. They'd come to something of an understanding.

Later, he pulled on a dark, light-weight jacket and walked. In less than half an hour, he was in Toppins. Striding across the bar, he hopped onto a bar stool. Eventually, he caught Mike's attention.

"You look awful." Mike didn't mince his words as he polished glasses. "Usual, Devan?" He momentarily closed his eyes. "No idea why I'm even asking." Throwing aside a bar towel, he picked a shot glass and half a bottle of bourbon from below the bar.

Devan grinned. "I feel terrible, yes. So that's why I look it," he said filling the shot glass and slinging it back. "And again, leave the-"

"I know," nodded Mike. He slid the bottle a little closer. "This is your bottle from when you had that God-awful cold. You paid for it, never finished it. Taxi or Aditi in town?"

"Taxi," replied Devan. "Please, and thank you. If you don't mind.

"Sure, but take it easy," Mike tapped the bottle. "There's no rush…."

"To get to the bottom," sighed Devan. "I know. Give me an hour, and then call a taxi. I promise to behave, even if Aditi…."

Mike frowned at him, there was distinct wariness. "One hour, Coultrie," he said firmly. "One hour."

Devan sunk a few more shots. He pushed Mike's hour by another forty-five minutes. Mike very diligently called a taxi. Devan wobbled across the bar and clambered into the back. Cracking a window, he rubbed his stomach. He didn't remember eating. The cab made it to the front of the house. As it sped away, Devan emptied his guts into the rose bushes by the porch.

Libby had been right. Drowning at the bottom of a bottle was never a good idea. Mentally kicking himself, Devan fumbled with his keys to get in. That took him a few attempts. He then had to negotiate the security system.

Devan Coultrie was drunk and in a seriously bad way.

Standing in the lounge, Devan looked at the space between the two windows. Positioned slap bang in the middle was a black and white photograph.

Him, Aditi; on their wedding day.

Wobbling forward, he grasped at the frame. Firming up his grip, Devan wrenched it free from the wall. Turning on his heel, he spun around to launch at the opposite wall. He heard the glass crack, the frame split at the corners. Shards of glass littered the carpet. What he saw before him, was his broken heart, his broken marriage with its vows turned to dust. He remembered joy in having found peace. Now it was all broken, battered and bruised.

He sadly shook his head. Devan had seen red. For the first time, in a long time, he had lost the plot. He knew that he shouldn't have touched the frame. That had been a mistake. The whole damned thing would have to be replaced.

Aditi would want to know.

If, she noticed.

If, she still cared.

Throwing his hands into the air, Devan conceded defeat. He really needed to go to bed. Trundling up the stairs, he got some water from the bathroom. Eventually, he clambered into bed. Suddenly, the bed felt too big, too empty and horribly cold.

□

# Chapter 7

Cardboard boxes. Devan was stood in a lift, holding onto them for dear life. He was only just able to look over the top. Each one was marked confidential, with the obligatory 'this way up'.

"This is all very exciting," Aditi grinned at him; she rubbed a smudge of lipstick away from his cheek. "We have a whole floor," she sounded excited; her tone was loaded with a sense of anticipation. "I even have my own office. This is big, Devan; it's massive."

With a clunky ding, the lift doors slid open at the sixth floor. Sign writers were busy hanging livery for the legal firm that Aditi worked for. The two of them gave Aditi and Devan a reverent nod as they walked out.

"Left a bit," Aditi waggled a finger, as she shepherded Devan through a set of heavy, double doors. "It's all coming together."

Devan kept his counsel, following his wife.

"We need to do some recruiting," she said, waving her hand at the open plan office. A handful of desks were scattered across a newly lain, slate-grey carpet.

Devan counted six desk chairs, all cocooned in protective, plastic covering. He looked up as strip lighting flickered to life.

"I don't miss this," he said, letting out a contented sigh. "I don't miss this one bit. You might want to think about pot plants," he added, following Aditi into an office.

"Noted," replied his wife. She even rolled her eyes.

Devan stuck out his tongue in retaliation. "Seriously," he declared, sounding very grave. "Call it employee welfare. No one wants to work in a concrete jungle. Where do you want these?" He didn't wait for an answer, dumping the boxes onto an expansive desk. Devan nearly took out a laptop and bulky looking 'phone.

"You owe me," he said, flexing his arms. He had no idea what he'd carried, but he felt the strain. "You've done good," he smiled as he watched Aditi shuffle around behind her desk. Her hand rested on the back of a swivel chair. Like the others outside, it was still covered in plastic.

From the corner of his eye, he espied another. High-backed, with dark wood arm-rests, it looked rather swanky.

Dragging it across, he slumped into it. Stretching out his legs, he crossed them at the ankle. Putting his hands behind his head, Devan sat in a peaceful repose.

He watched Aditi, she watched him. He could see worry etched across her face. All of her earlier excitement had dissipated away. She'd barely slept last night. She'd come home, unexpectedly. This morning she had asked if fancied going for a drive, coming here with boxes.

Devan also saw something else. He saw vulnerability, painted across her brow.

Aditi was scared. He could see it, feel it too. A tight knot had formed in the middle of his stomach.

"Have I," she asked, finally breaking the silence. "Have I really done good? It was one hell of a risk, walking away from everything in England. To start up again here in Billings. It's very scary."

"I know," his words came out softly, reassuringly. "It'll all be worth it, though." He inclined his head, to beckon her over.

Floating away from the desk, Aditi landed in his lap. Her legs dangled across his, only just grazing the floor.

Drawing her close, Devan smiled as her elbows nudged into his shoulders. His arms curled around her waist, he inhaled the heady scent of her perfume. Today, was a rose and vanilla day.

"Risk is what keeps us alive," he drew circles across her stomach. "It keeps us on our toes," he bit his lip as Aditi fiddled with his hair. "Risk is what keeps things interesting. Risk," Devan pressed his forehead against Aditi's, to nudge her nose. "With romance, is even better." He was unable to add any more as Aditi took his lips hostage. He surrendered completely, willing to pay her ransom.

This was what he missed, what he desperately craved with every inch of his being. Moments like this, Aditi was all his. She was there; heart, body and soul. He could and would surrender every inch of his being, to have her wrapped up in his arms.

"We're in this together," he dabbed a finger onto a stray eyelash that had strayed on the apple of his wife's cheek. "You're not doing this alone. I wouldn't have it for one. We're a partnership, a team. What we do, we do hand-in-hand, together."

Cradling his face, Aditi smothered him with kisses. Yet, she still looked a little on edge.

He knew why. He knew exactly what she was hiding. Devan could see it in her eyes, and every time he dared to look.

"What we have, Aditi," he felt his stomach flip as he said her name. "Is worth more than can be found in heaven, on earth and in between. I like it, more than I will ever be able to say, and want to live a whole lifetime, holding onto it. Aditi Rao, you are my whole world."

Then he saw it. Aditi's bottom lip had started to tremble. She been pouting at first, but the quiver grew. It had been gentle at first, almost seductive. Soon, the quaking spread to the rest of her. Every inch of Aditi hummed. Devan felt her relax and fall apart in his arms. Aditi's head fell onto his shoulders; he ran a hand gently down her spine. He felt her every sinew pull taut at the prospect of doing this alone.

"You're not alone," he uttered, stroking her hair. "You'll never be alone."

This wasn't about Chris. For once, this had nothing to do with him.

Devan had seen her fear, her trepidation. She was a young, successful woman, charged with setting up a legal practice, miles from where she had called home. Their marriage, telegraphic as it was, was part of larger picture.

"I'm so sorry," he whispered gently, not wanting to make things worse. "I should've seen this sooner. I'll do all I can, to stand by you, help you. Like I'm supposed to; as your husband, that's my job. I should be there, at all costs. I'm all yours, Aditi. I always will be."

He could hear Aditi shift, her face pressed against his shirt. Then there was the rather laboured breathing as her chest rose and fell against his. She held onto him tightly; more tightly than he had ever experienced.

They sat for a while. Aditi was a puddle in his arms. All he could do was catch her, hold her close. Eventually, she stopped shaking. He'd felt the stress and anxiety drift away. Aditi took her time sliding off his lap and to her feet.

Devan was given a tour of the sixth floor. They'd drunk some really bad tea in the kitchen of the breakroom. Recruitment would give her the staff to use it properly.

"You'll need a secretary," he said, removing a tea bag from his mug to drop it into a waste bin. "Or personal assistant. Whatever they call it over here. They will have to know my birthday, what presents to buy me. Which opera tickets to hunt down, should we ever have a fight. My inside leg too, when you want to buy me something nice."

Devan and Aditi were sat at Formica table, their drinks positioned between them. Aditi's hand was sat upon his. She was absent-mindedly fiddling with his wedding ring.

"I'll want full disclosure," he commented. "Secretary, I have no problem with. It's the personal, followed by assistant that alarms me." He winked as he picked up his tea.

"You're funny," Aditi couldn't have been more deadpan, her eyes narrowed at him. Her eyeliner had smudged to accent the pink tinge of her eyes. She'd cried her heart and soul out into his arms. "I'll put out an ad, asking for one of the seven dwarves."

"Make it an ogre," Devan retorted. "One that lives below a bridge. One of those, I could deal with. God, this tea is awful." He made no bones as he pulled a face. "This flat in Billings. The one that the firm gave you. You said you wanted to show me." She made reference to it, and now wanted him to see it. See where she stayed, when not on Oakview.

The flat. In his head, it was something of a crime scene. The place, where Aditi flouted her marriage vows.

Slinging back her tea, Aditi grimaced. "That *is* bad. Yeah, of course," she said, nodding. "There's better tea there, for one. More boxes too, actually. Let's go," she added, picking up the mugs and moving to the sink. "You can take down the particulars, if you want; mine too." Aditi winked at him, as though she had a plan.

Devan actually blushed. He felt his cheeks burn. He'd had worse offers.

Twenty minutes later, Devan stood at a window. Barefoot, he looked out at the sprawling mass that was Billings. In his hands, was a mug of well-brewed, beautifully strong, English Breakfast tea. This flat, was a whole forty-five minutes from his own. As he drank the tea, he convinced himself that the timing was adequate. The town was big enough for two illicit rendezvous places.

Looking at his feet, he slid his toes through a very thick, very luxuriously deep-piled carpet. The whole place was sumptuous. In the master bedroom, there was massive great big sleigh bed. That was where he had been dragged as soon as Aditi had opened the door. That was where Aditi had stayed whilst he made tea.

Neither one of them smoked. Tea was the done thing.

He had kept calm, made tea. It had felt like the right thing to do.

As returned to the vista of Billings, a pair of arms snaked around his ribcage.

"Tea okay?" she asked, her hands travelled to the bottom of his shirt to then press against his skin.

"Lovely," replied Devan, turning to face her.

"Thank you," she said; her heart thudded against him. He could feel the rise and fall, as her curves and contours made themselves known.

"Don't tell me," he pressed his lips against the soft hollow below her jaw.

"I'll just show you," she finished his sentence for him. Snatching his hand, she once more dragged him to the sleigh bed.

He took his tea with him.

The next time that Devan went to Aditi's flat, there was purpose rather than pleasure. All because he wanted to expand his Hooch Baron empire.

"Don't shave so close," Aditi beseeched. Jeweled bangles jangled and glistened at her wrists.

"Yes, dear," Devan muttered. His jaw jutted out as his brass razor passed through shaving cream. This was a precision job, done slowly but surely. Three days worth of stubble was being done away with. He moved his gaze from Aditi's reflection to focus on his own.

"And did you have to cut your hair so short," He saw Aditi plant her hands on her hips. Dunking his razor, he span around to face her. Devan was ready to scream and shout.

Only she was standing there in stockings, suspenders and what looked like a well-engineered Basque. He took his time, absorbing the view. His eyes wandered, as though he was already taking it all off.

"Stop," Aditi waggled a finger. "It took me nearly forty minutes to get into this stuff. Will take you just as long to get me out of it." The smile that had spread across her ruby lips was echoing what was going through his mind.

"Later then," he said, turning back to his reflection. "What dress you going for?" he yelled, she'd scarpered off.

"What do you fancy?" she yelled back, having gone into the bedroom.

"RED!" he replied. "Everyone wears black to these things, even the women. Make a statement. You're the wife of a Hooch Baron." As he finished off, he heard Aditi cackle.

Two days ago, they'd driven to Billings on a shopping trip. This evening was a gala dinner, and his wife suddenly decided that she didn't have a stitch to wear.

That was what he planned to tell his accountant too.

Three dresses later, he felt as though he was doing the whole Hooch Baron thing some justice.

Rubbing his face dry, he dabbed a few blobs of cocoa butter onto the red raw of a close shave. He winced at the sting. Devan swept a fop of hair back. After years of wearing it long, he'd hacked most of it off. Looking once more at his reflection, he doubled checked for any signs of crow's feet.

For now, he was okay.

He fiddled with his hair again. As much as he liked being a Hooch Baron, looking like one and from a novella made him feel slightly uneasy. Aditi had pouted and protested as he had sat in the barber's chair. He'd been dragged around all of the dress stores. The least she could do, was put up with a haircut.

Padding into Aditi's bedroom, Devan sat on the edge of her sleigh bed. A pair of dresses were hung by the dresser. Draped across them, were a pair of blue and pink polka-dotted socks. One by one, he put them on.

On the far side, Aditi stepped into a vermillion-coloured gown. It had a sweetheart neckline that gave way to a drop waist. He got to his feet, having struggled to sit on his hands. He simply had to help.

"Take a deep breath," he pulled her close from behind.

"Before you take it away?" came the reply.

"Maybe later," Devan negotiated a zip. Then came a series of buttons that he couldn't imagine tearing off in a hurry.

He knew exactly how much the dress was worth.

As Aditi leant against him, he drew circles across her stomach.

"Devan…." She was away with the faeries, and then some. She turned slowly to face him.

"Now," Aditi tip toed, her lips landed kiss across his neck. "Take my breath away. Now."

He undid the zip. He took care of the buttons.

They had more than forty minutes. The wine reception could wait.

When the car service had arrived, Devan had vaulted out of the sleigh bed. The socks had gone back on; he'd bundled on his dress shirt. His tuxedo was pulled on, in a frenzy. Aditi had left her flat dressed in a robe. Her vermillion gown hung over one arm, make up in her hand. She'd fallen into the car, Devan behind her. He'd thrown her shoes in after her.

Jabbing at the partition, Devan watched his wife get dressed for the second time. He made a mental note to never again buy her such complicated underwear.

Simple knickers never got in the way.

□

# Chapter 8

He'd been out like a light. Deep in a dreamless slumber, Devan didn't register the movement that came from his bed being invaded. Accustomed to having the cavernous space to himself, he used the whole space from the middle. He saw nothing wrong with being spread-eagled across the bed.

"Oi, move over," That immediately made him worry. Covers were pushed away to let in cold air.

For all of twenty seconds, Devan wondered who was about to fall into his bed. Which woman, and more specifically, what did she want? All he wanted was to sleep. Devan had spent the whole day wrangling with his Hooch Baron empire. He was in no mood to play nice, regardless of whoever was about to slide in alongside him.

"Devan, it's me," Aditi coiled in close around him. Sliding an elastic band from around her wrist, she pulled her dark locks into a ponytail. "Aditi, your wife, and not The Spanish Armada. Stand down, this isn't an invasion."

"Could've fooled me," he said, making no effort to stifle a long yawn. "Hello, how you doing?" he asked, blinking to refocus. "Did you remember that I exist?" he asked, rubbing his eyes.

"I didn't forget," Aditi ran a toe along his legs, swamping him completely. "You make a lovely sleeping beauty," her words were punctuated by splodgy kisses landing wherever she could reach.

"Flattery will get you everywhere," he closed his eyes, tilted his head back and let his wife do whatever she wanted to. "Sleep with me," he said, feeling the tug of the covers. "In my arms, as though I was the only boy in the world."

There was a murmur of disappointment. Aditi pouted, threw his pajama bottoms out of the bed.

Devan fixed her with a glare that could've passed for smoulder.

Relenting, she settled back into his arms.

There was closeness, the warmth of Aditi's body; each and every inch buffered the truth.

He wasn't the only boy in the world. Yet for the next few hours, he held onto it. He held on to Aditi as though she were the only girl in the world. He knew better though. Two, could play at that game.

In the morning, base instinct kicked in. With his arms empty, Devan awoke to fling out a limb towards where Aditi should have been. When she wasn't to be found, his heart leapt into mouth.

Had he dream it, had he imagined it all? Had she really been here? Throwing back covers, Devan was starting to question everything.

"Aditi?" he called out, waiting; listening for the slightest movement.

He couldn't have drunk dreamt it. Perhaps now was a good time to ditch the bourbon. That's said, it had been weeks, maybe two, since he had last downed anything significant.

Cautiously, Devan swung his feet to the floor. The line that existed between reality and fantasy had become invisible, rather than just blurry.

"Aditi Rao, are you here?" Devan yelled this time. He needed to know if he was going mad and to what extent.

"Yes!" The reply was shrill, a little panicked. "In here. Come here a minute would you."

The bathroom; Aditi was in the bathroom. Getting to his feet, Devan ran in the direction of her voice. He wasn't going mad; not yet, anyway.

"Please don't drag me into your shower," he said, opening the door. There she was. Sat upon the toilet; half a dozen pregnancy tests scattered across the floor. A seventh was in her hands. Aditi was staring at it intently; as though willing it to change.

Devan held his breath as she looked up. His brows had gone up; he tried to lower them immediately. What he felt was anticipation. Dreaded anticipation, his stomach had flipped.

That was not a good sign.

"False alarm," she half-whispered the result. Her face was a pale, accentuating the dark circles below her eyes.

For now, all she carried was guilt.

Devan let out sigh of relief. His heart had been sat somewhat precariously in his mouth. Slowly, it descended back to its rightful place. He was rooted to the spot, with no clue as to what he was meant to do next. Something profound hung between them. Something so electric; it was strained and painfully hard to grapple with.

"Next time," he couldn't think of anything else to say. He saw the colour slowly return to Aditi's face. A soft flush, as though she was thawing out.

Walking into the bathroom, Devan felt the cold of the tiles below his feet. Lowering himself to his knees, he scooped up the tests to throw them into a swing-lidded garbage bin. Holding out his hand, he wanted the last one.

It landed in his hand- a negative-and was launched into the garbage.

Aditi's gaze was pinned upon him. She wore an expression of disbelief married to curiosity.

"We should talk," her eyes dipped away to the floor.

"Stick the kettle on." Getting to his feet, Devan washed his hands. Aditi stepped forwards from the toilet seat to do the same. He found his toothbrush, applied paste. He'd take his time, shower first, and then go downstairs. He did exactly that, approximately twenty minutes later. When Devan got to the lounge, there was toast and tea on the coffee table. It was half past eleven, and well beyond breakfast. There had been a lie in, having spent the wee hours in the throes of pure passion.

Aditi sat on the sofa, waiting.

"Devan, are we ready?" she picked up her tea, cradled it in her palms. "Having kids is a big deal. There'd have to be some big changes."

Striding towards the sofa, Devan picked up his tea to sit down. He had a feeling, to simply listen.

"I'd need to stay here, in The States," continued Aditi. "Which should be easier, with the office in Billings done. Do we need to worry about citizenship, would it be better if we had kids back in Britain? I mean, think of the accents."

He half-snorted at the last bit. This, this was what worried her?

"Flip me," Devan scratched at his ear. "Easy there, sweetheart. One thing at a time. Let's just make them first, these kids. That bit's fairly fun. All of rest, we can worry about later. You're over thinking this, you really are."

"Do you want to have children, and with me?" Aditi shuffled to face him.

"Yes," he said. Turning toward her, Devan stopped thinking about toast. "This isn't a case of if either, but when. You took seven pregnancy tests, Aditi."

"Nine," she replied. "I took two at the office. Came home to you with a bagful; I had to make sure."

Something hit his radar, and hard. "What about you?" he asked, his brows knitted together. "Do you want babies...."Devan's heart raced a little. "And with me? Only you sound scared, conflicted too. Overthinking it, is that your way of telling me no?"

He watched her face blanche once more. Her hands had settled on his.

"What is it?" he asked, he had to press further. "Tell me," Devan urged, "Tell me what's going on?" A hot, fiery ball of pain was building in his gut. It wasn't fear, but fury. He could also feel the warmth of Aditi's fingers. Fingers that were now very sweaty. He moved his fingers, to her wrist. Her pulse was quick, frantic; it met his in a weird synchronicity.

Aditi gulped, passed her tongue across dry lips.

This wasn't about words. Devan could see that in her eyes; tears had formed. Letting go of her hand, he wiped away those that fell down her cheeks.

"Go," whispered Devan, "Leave," he added, putting his hands into his lap. "We're not ready," he felt his own tears descend. "We can't do this yet. Not if you feel this way, and about a false alarm. We have to be on the same page, on the same path. Right now, that's two different pages, two different paths. Come back; find me, when you're ready. I'll be right here." He slid across the sofa; drawing in his arms and legs, he holed himself into the corner. Devan buried his head into his arms.

He didn't see her leave; he heard the sniffs and sobs. There was the clattering around upstairs, with no goodbye as the front door thumped closed. Aditi's car revved noisily; the brakes screeched as she left.

This was their parting. This was their ending.

Their paths would have to re-join.

Hopefully.

□

# Chapter 9

To be alone, it all hurt too much. He wasn't going to sit at home and sulk. Oakview once more felt too big and overwhelming. The walls felt as though they were closing in, trapping him in misery. He had to escape. Eventually, Devan got off the sofa, drank his tea, put on his shoes and socks.

Then he made a 'phone call.

Getting into his car, he slung a black hold-all into the back. He turned the key in the ignition, put his foot down and headed out of Peace.

A shattered peace.

There was only place that he wanted to be. Only one person that he wanted.

Thankfully, she was available.

Driving to Billings was all very blurry around the edges. Devan parked in the space allocated to the apartment to head on up. Stale air hit him in the face as he opened the door. The curtains were drawn; everything was shrouded secrecy and darkness. Spontaneity and sex might as well have hung from the ceiling in pink neon.

The apartment did its job. Nothing more, mothing less. That was always the arrangement. Dumping his bag in the bedroom, he pulled out half a bottle of bourbon. In the kitchen, he found two glasses.

He took a seat in the lounge, filling both glasses.

Sex and Spontaneity.

Nothing more, nothing less.

It didn't take her long to arrive. He'd downed one drink at that point.

Devan heard the lock click; the door silently swept open. He heard her handbag land with a thud on the carpet. Shoes were kicked off next, hitting the wall.

Her fingers pressed against his cheeks; her lips brushed against his.

There were worse ways to say hello. Devan's resistance was practically non-existent as he pulled her around and into his lap.

She had screamed and squealed. His name was flung repeatedly at the walls. He didn't say a word, he didn't half to. His fingers did all the talking for him. Moving deftly to undo buttons, tease away a zipper; unhook a fairly uncomplicated bra.

Uncomplicated. That, he liked.

It was the stockings that made him smile. He took great pleasure in rolling them off and away.

Melissa arched back on the sofa, halfway to unbridled, unadulterated ecstasy.

Suspenders pinged away easily, without protest.

The coffee table was shunted away, dust flew as it moved. There was only so much that the sofa could take. On the floor, there were elbows, arms and legs. Everything moved apace; anger, arousal and adrenaline combined all too well.

This was it. One last time.

They wouldn't make it as far as the bedroom.

It was dawn before Devan decided to retreat to Peace. He sat in the kitchen, sipping water whilst in his boxers and socks. He knew exactly what he had to do. Melissa covered every inch of his skin. Her scent mingled with salt and sweat. Devan had reveled in it all. This was the first time that he felt dirty. As though he needed to shower or shed his skin. Every inch of him, tingled with infidelity. For the first time, this all hit home.

"I bought you those socks," her voice hit the back of his neck. His palms pressed against his shoulder. Her every curve made itself known as she leant against his back. "The boxers too. Seemed a fair exchange for the stockings and suspenders. Expenses."

His resistance was painfully thin as he closed his eyes.

"Please don't turn me on," he said, sliding her hands away. He knew exactly what her hands were capable of. Slowly, he got up from the bar stool where he had perched. He turned around, pulling Melissa's hips close. Devan sandwiched his feet either side of hers.

"You've had enough," she said, tracing a line across his cheek. "You don't' want to do this anymore. This is it; you want to call time."

He nodded, as he looked into the depths of her eyes. There were flecks of light blue on the outer rims that he'd never noticed before.

"I have to be your accountant again," Melissa drew in a breath. "Not something to be written off. I'm losing you, to her. To the woman, you pretend to love. The woman, who pretends to love you, yet messes around with someone else."

"I can't judge," whispered Devan. "I'm doing the same; that makes me no better. I can't be that man, not anymore. I'm bigger, better, than that."

"Bigger, better?" Melissa tutted in disbelief. "Then her, or the man she's sleeping with? She lost you ages ago. Why go back, why take her back?"

"Because I can," he replied, "Because, I want to; as it's all I know, all I want. I love her, for having loved me when I'd forgotten what the damned word meant."

"And me?" Melissa blinked; her eye lashes cast dark shadows across her skin. "Was I toy, a game to be played when you felt like it? To be tinkered and toyed with, put back when you were done? Disposable, I guess."

Shaking his head, Devan pressed his forehead against hers. Cradling her face, he conceded one last, long lingering kiss. One last taste of something that frayed the edges of his soul.

"You were sunshine in the darkness," he said softly. "A light when I needed it the most; when I was lost, alone and hurt. Never disposable; ever."

Melissa slid free from his arms. Briefly their fingers remained inter-twined, before untangling apart.

He let it linger. So much so, he didn't see the open palm impact across his face. Melissa sprinted away, a blur in his daze. A hot flush flared across his face; his ears felt as though they were ringing.

Devan heard fumbling in the lounge, the heavy thud of the door closing.

One last time.

It was all over.

□

# Chapter 10

There was little point in keeping the apartment. It was no longer necessary, all things considered. He left just as the clock struck noon, having showered. Devan removed every trace of Melissa that had been daubed across his skin. His socks and boxers were unceremoniously removed to be dumped into the garbage. It was the start of a purge; he had few things at Oakview that needed to go as well.

Melissa had been both a vice and a demon. Both aspects needed to be cleansed. You could excise a vice, rub it out. Demons were different.

She wasn't, however, the only demon.

That would take time.

The first stage was going into the Realtors. He'd gone in, given notice. He'd have it cleaned, reset. Devan didn't need it anymore; it had served its purpose. The keys would be posted back, there were two sets. He handed Melissa's over, there and then. There wasn't so much as a second glance.

Times were a-changing.

Slinking his hands into his pockets, Devan walked down the street toward the parking lot. There was no room on the busy street, this side of Billings. Feeling the breeze nip at his ears, Devan pulled up his collar. His jacket was a little thin; there was a bite on the breeze. The cold however, was the least of his problems.

Devan took his time as he walked; he was in no real hurry.

Only he saw something. A figure dressed in blue. A shadow.

Lowering his shoulders, Devan picked up his pace. His strides lengthened as he moved closer. Closer, towards someone he hadn't expected to stumble upon.

Not here. Not in Montana.

Weaving in and out pedestrians, he moved with fast fury. Sharp apologies littered his movement as he made his way.

"Devan Coultrie. We-."

He threw the first punch.

Quick, hard and then grabbed the man by his shoulder.

Christopher Feltham was bundled into an alley by a Chinese restaurant. Bundled out of the way, and in broad daylight.

In the darkness, blows rained, casting shadows on the walls. Devan's oxblood Dr. Martens squeaked and scuffed across concrete. In the darkness, a duel was fought. Two wills squared up to each other, full to the brim with bile and defiance.

Both parties grumbled and groaned. Fists flews, kicks lashed out. Blood was spilled.

Ten minutes later, Devan exited the alley. Reaching into his pocket, he pulled out a pale blue handkerchief. Dabbing it across his face, he spat out blood. There was even a broken tooth. He peered at his reflection in the window of the restaurant. His nose was scratched, his eyes would come up bruised something beautiful in the morning. There was an angry, red raw gash across his jaw. Devan continued to dab haphazardly at this face, trying to mop the wounds of war.

A war; this had only been a battle.

Tucking away the handkerchief, he made his way to the car.

Getting back to Oakview was relatively easy. Devan drove as though he was on autopilot, in silence. There was no playlist today. He kept his eyes on the road, hands on the wheel. He was holding on tightly; his knuckles smarted under strain. His skin was cut, grazed; smudges of blood may it all look worse than it was.

With every breath, Devan felt his ribs twang beneath his shirt. He had taken pretty much as good as he had given. Chris had little more bulk to him; he was heavier set than Devan. In comparison, Devan had been lighter, more fluid on his feet. He'd taken pride in being able to land bigger, better, more precise body blows.

Devan had left Chris in the alley, sliding down the wall. He'd not so much as looked backward or thought about the potential consequences. The street had been busy; he'd shoved Chris in to the alley to be able to control things. That was the only element for which Devan had actively engaged his brain.

Checking his rear-view mirror, Devan finally thought about it. There'd probably be consequences. Assault, maybe even disturbing the peace. He could have walked away; ignored Chris, let things unravel differently. If he' done that, there wouldn't have been any blood.

Devan scoffed loudly and laughed. His bruised face wasn't best pleased.

A cow would've jumped over the moon, before Devan would have left that man alone. Pigs would've started to fly.

He was always going to knock three shades of yellow, out of Chris Feltham.

It would take the best part of a week for Devan's cuts and bruises to heal. His knuckles calmed down; moving from angry, red and raw to fleshy pink. His ribs stopped roaring with every breath too. Fortunately, nothing was broken. Through pure dumb luck, there were just bruises. No part of him wondered, cared or wanted to know what state Chris was in. The thought hadn't crossed his mind once.

Aditi had been gone a week too, just over in fact. This time, her absence felt different. It was amplified, echoing louder and harder around Oakview.

He'd woken up that morning and decided to strip the bed. Sheet, duvet, blanket; it was all taken off, thrown into the laundry hamper. Devan had stood at the foot of the bed,

The Marital Bed.

His, hers; shared.

Moving to Aditi's side, he had sat down in the middle.

"What if she doesn't come back," he asked out aloud. "She might have chosen me once, but will she choose me again."

Devan curled his fingers around the edge of the mattress. The stupid thing was horribly hard on her side. The one side that was barely occupied.

"Oh, shut up!" he yelled, his words bounced back from the walls. "Woe is you, yes; but what are you going to do about it. Plus, it's too damned early for bourbon."

Devan leapt to his feet.

"Can't be sitting here all day," he hauled the hamper into his arms, and headed downstairs. He thundered around the laundry, picking a fight with his washing machine.

Then came breakfast.

Sipping tea, he nibbled at toast. Aditi was everywhere he looked. Thanksgiving, Christmas, even Valentine's Day, had all centered on his kitchen. Of all the places that evoked happy memories, the kitchen sucker -punched him sideways.

As he cried, his mug fell to the floor. Tea landed in a starburst across the tiles. The mug, a goner, smashed to smithereens.

The whole damned thing was empty. Empty, cold and absent of Aditi. She had made this place feel like a home. Without her, Oakview was a shell, haunted by sadness and devoid of joy. There was no heart, no soul; no bliss, whatsoever.

Slowly, Devan sank to the floor, to land upon his knees. Curled up, Devan Coultrie sobbed as his fragmented soul became nothing but ribbons.

Every inch of him hurt. Every inch of him throbbed, in desire. Every sinew wanted her.

He wanted, Aditi.

An hour passed, then two. Devan eventually unfurled himself from the foetal position. It took time and effort to organise his limbs, to get to his feet.

"This is probably what cold turkey feels like," he let out a pained, animalistic groan. He wiped off his face with a damp red and white tea-towel. Devan had produced enough phlegm and bogey to sink a small ship.

"I don't want to go cold turkey," Devan declared, throwing the tea-towel to the floor. He went back down to his knees; the tea was mopped up. The broken mug was scooped up, dropped into the garbage. "You don't go cold turkey from your wife, from the woman you love," he snorted and sniffed, wiping away a few random, remaining tears. "This isn't over," he yelled, screwing the tea-towel up and launching it into the sink.

Devan needed space, time and air. A walk into town would do it, perhaps a table in Sheila's. He'd get some pancakes, sit and do some people watching.

Sheila's; that place was a refuge.

Pancakes would be morsels to mend his soul.

It was still too damned early to hit the bourbon.

The minute that he stepped into Sheila's, Devan saw Laura. She had been one of the first people he had met in Peace. When he had first arrived to pick up the keys to Oakview, she'd been his server. Since then, Sheila's had become a big part of his life.

"Take a seat," she nodded towards an empty table. "I'll be right over with your coffee and pancakes. Just give me two minutes."

Devan mustered up a weak smile. It really wasn't his best work. He took a seat at the table, falling wearily onto the chair. Over time, he and Laura had established a fairly good, working relationship. Skulking around Sheila's was more than a habit. The diner had become a home from home. Sat with his back to the wall, Devan looked out the window.

"I forgot to say. Thank you," Laura was super quick with his coffee as she appeared at his elbow. "For all that information you gave me about investment bonds. It really helped to sort out what to do with my inheritance."

"A pleasure," replied Devan, watching as his coffee cup was filled three-quarters of the way. "Now just make sure that you find a proper school to spend it on, Laura. Not some Mickey Mouse place. You have a beautiful brain," he said picking up the coffee. "Don't waste that either."

Laura blushed; nervously, she twirled a lock of hair at her shoulder. At her lobe, a blue-stoned stud glimmered in the sunlight.

"I'll try," there was a rather coquettish smile, a light nod. "I'll get your pancakes. Strawberries and syrup, right? We might even have some of those raspberries that you grew."

"That would be lovely." Devan tried to smile again. Only his muscles, brain and heart were, after all, woefully disconnected. Plus, having taken punches didn't help.

Laura left, leaving Devan to sulk into his coffee. He put the cup down to dose it with sugar. Sheila's was yet to figure out tea.

"Jay told me you might be here," The voice cracked across his sulk. Devan snapped his neck to look up. "Well, he made an educated guess; I took a chance."

A plate of pancakes clunked on the table. His wife slid it across towards him.

"Jericho called me too," Aditi's gaze was trained to run straight through him. Her lashes all fanned out, heightening the drama. "The boys haven't seen hide not hair of you in a week. You could've been hit by a bus, for all they knew. Haven't responded to their calls, their messages; not answering the damned door. They were worried…. I got worried too."

Aditi plonked her 'phone onto the table.

"You thought of me then?" Devan heard himself squeak, rather than speak. Gingerly, his hand slid across the table towards Aditi's. Their fingertips touched as though a scared kiss. He felt his wedding band spin around his finger.

"I think of you all the time," Aditi's tone was low, but level. "Every hour, every day and every moment. I think about you, about how much you deserve to be loved, to be happy. I think about how I promised to do that, and so far, I've failed."

A tear formed at the corner of Aditi's right eye. It travelled down the side of her nose, to land on the curve of her top lip.

"All those promises, Devan," Aditi's words had become a whisper. "I broke them, and God, I wish; I wish that I could mend them."

He let out a gasp, his heart felt that much heavier. This hurt, just as much as the empty kitchen. Devan was also little confused. He had heard what sounded like a confession. This was a confession in all but name.

"Come home," he said, enveloping her hand in his. "Come back to me, I promise we can mend. We can fix this, it's not all kaput." Devan licked away a tears he didn't know had started.

He saw Aditi gulp; he saw something flicker in her eyes as she took her hand away. From the corner of his eye, he saw that Laura was watching. Then there was the sound of Mrs. Johnson on the other side of the diner. She was talking loudly, about him and Aditi. He heard another sound, there was buzzing. Aditi's 'phone hopped around as it vibrated. He flicked his gaze towards the device, hoping that it wasn't Chris. That would have damned well sent him over the edge.

"It's Rohan," sniffed Aditi, answering the call and put it on loudspeaker.

"It's a boy!!" screamed Rohan, his barely concealed excitement felt like a torrent across the line. "Where's my brother, the useless numpty isn't answering his bloody 'phone. Aditi, I've got a son. Tell him."

"He's here," she kicked Devan under the table. Their moment had been smashed, volleyed away into the long grass.

"Congrat-Congratulations!" His throat had clammed up, and he struggled to speak. "Sorry, my phone's- Congratulations. All okay? I mean, Libby, you, the baby? How much did he weigh in at?" Devan was all very disorientated.

"Yes, yes; nine pounds four," Rohan was bouncing on the other side of the world. "Both resting, Hang up, I need to call the grandparents. I'll call you later. Make sure you pick up, wazzock."

The line went dead; Aditi took the device away. Once more, it was just the two of them.

"Call the boys," Aditi turned the tables back. "Tell them that you're alive. They were genuinely worried. They care about you."

"And you?" He felt compelled to ask. "What about you?"

He watched as Aditi rose from her seat. She zipped up her coat, slunk her hands into the pockets. Devan saw more tears start to stream; her eyes were awfully pink. He felt the sharp searing pain; his own and hers.

Devan could hear Mrs. Johnson witter on still. She sounded as though she was giving a commentary; she uttered his and Aditi's names as though this was football.

"Whilst you're here," ventured Aditi, wiping away tears. "I'm going to pop into Oakview. I want to take Pudding. I miss her, she's my baby."

"Until we have our own?" Devan couldn't resist. "One without four legs and fur."

"Don't rush home," she stated; a poker face reforming. "Eat your pancakes, call the boys. Your parents too. You and I have a new-born nephew."

With that, Aditi slopped off out the door.

# Chapter 11

A gulf had formed between them. It was too deep, too wide. He and Aditi couldn't have been more poles apart. Devan had thought about it for days after. She had taken her cat. He'd done his best to look after Pudding; he held nothing against the fur ball, not really.

As for the boys, Devan remained in hermit mode. There was no desire to reach out, to communicate with anyone. Another week went by fairly quickly. He pottered around Oakview, leaving only to go to Brightman's to stock up on essentials.

Devan Coultrie had become the ghost of a man. He was a spectre; gliding here and there, whilst in a pained world of his own. Only he couldn't keep that up for long.

On the far side of Billings, the local business association had scheduled a black-tie event. As the local hooch baron, Devan had received an invitation from one the insiders. The associate in question was a fairly big mover and shaker; they'd taken something of a special interest. He used the flat for one last time. It seemed the most appropriate thing to do.

First, there was another haircut. Sat in the barber's chair, Devan zoned out avoid his reflection. He'd become accustomed to a short back and sides. Gone were the days of locks that snaked towards his collar. Besides, no one was around to tease, tousle or run her fingers through it. The kinks and curls had only ever been good for that one thing. He'd resisted having it cut, fiddled with, for such a long time. Devan was now relieved; all the weight and thickness was gone. He may have felt Vampiric in his own company, but he wouldn't look it in the company of others.

Arriving at the flat, he showered; carefully avoided the pomade that made his newly shorn locks glisten. He made sure the flat was tidy enough to be handed back, as he dusted in his sock and boxers. Then came the suit carrier suspended from the bedroom door. The zipper burred as he pulled out his tuxedo. He'd last worn it a few months ago. Devan made a mental note to find another one, for whatever the Hooch Baron Persona got into next. He had something of a character to play. Devan smiled wolfishly as he ran a finger down a lapel.

Devan Coultrie the Hooch Baron, was a rather interesting character to play. He could be smooth, suave, all very unassuming when he wanted to be. Yet, he was also capable of being a complete and utter tosspot if the circumstances warranted it. Years of working in The City of London had paid off in ways that Devan had never dreamt of as being useful.

He spent the next hour getting into character. Standing in the bathroom, he pulled on the crisp, white, dress shirt that had cost half a kidney. It had white, mother of pearl buttons that glinted on the harsh light. As he buttoned up, he could smell the scent of the citrus that the dry cleaners used to mask their weapons. Going into the bedroom, he found cufflinks to fasten his sleeves. Sat on the nightstand, these were chrome ovals, engraved with his initials. Sleeves fastened, he spritzed on cologne. He didn't want to honk halfway to hell, and of citrus.

Devan took off his wedding ring and sat it next to the box that had contained the cuff links.

Next came his trousers; dense, but crisp and creased down the front for prestige. You could have cut an orange on the front. Shoes were sought, from beneath the bed. These were new, shiny and very spiffy looking. Devan had grated the soles. There was nothing quite like going head over heels, after one too many. Plus, there would probably be dancing tonight. New shoes and a dance floor could make tripping the light fantastic a bit difficult.

His cummerbund was sat on his pillows. Devan tied it around his waist; it felt a little loose at first. He tugged it tighter on the second set of hooks and eyes. Last but not least, Devan pulled on his jacket. His tie was tucked into the breast pocket, behind a scarlet handkerchief. Unfurling the bow, he tweaked that into place. Satisfied, that he looked almost decent, Devan made for the door. He knew the night could have an interesting ending. With foresight, he'd booked a car service to take him. A Hooch Baron was supposed to arrive in style, and somewhat at his leisure. If he was going to a do job, he was inclined to do it properly.

Set on the outskirts of Billings, a faux country pile was the stage for the black-tie event. In the back of the car, Devan had time to contemplate his fate. He had been debating how drunk he could get, knowing that he had lift back to the flat. A mile out from the estate, Devan caught sight of a car pulled over. The bonnet steamed. He knew that car.

"Hey, pull over behind," he said, looking at the driver in the rear view. "We've got room for another."

The driver complied, edging the dark blue saloon over towards a narrow verge.

"I'll be two minutes," Devan hopped out, keeping the door open. Avoiding mud and grass, he picked his way towards the passenger side of the second car. Looking inside, he tapped the window.

Slowly the window whirred down. He inhaled deeply.

"Hello, stranger," he said, smiling somewhat uneasily. "Don't suppose you need a ride. I have room for a little one."

That mile felt like it went on forever. Silence was strung taut in the back of the saloon. For every yard, Devan heard his heart race as blood rushed around his ears. Once the car pulled up, he hopped out to open the door for the second passenger. There was some part of his Hooch Baron Persona that was actually a gentleman.

Dressed in bottle green, Melissa glided out. She wore a metallic sheened, sheath dress that went in and out in all the right places. The spike heels that she wore lengthened her legs to make her look like a Goddess. The curve of Melissa's calves had been a source of great pleasure. He knew all her curves, inch by inch. In and out.

"You just couldn't resist, could you?" Melissa put her hand to his. "Of all the dark streets to be rescued on, you just had to be on the same one."

Devan offered his arm instead. "Well," he said, rolling his shoulders to shrug. "You looked too sad, too pretty, to be left waiting for a tow truck."

Melissa scoffed as she rolled her eyes. "For a pickup line, Devan, that's awful," she held his arm a little tighter as walked up stairs to the front door. "And room for a little one?"

"I know," sighed Devan. "There's nothing little about you."

And so the evening began.

For the most part, Melissa dangled from Devan's arm. There was, after all, networking to done, by both of them. Pressing the flesh and schmoozing would do no harm his Hooch Baron Empire.

At dinner, it was only a place setting that separated them; some self-control, as well. Devan sat on his hands; his fingers almost turned blue.

With the band striking up after, Devan found himself on the dance floor. Melissa just happened to be in his arms as they moved to the rhythm of a double base and some rather seductive swing.

"You're not wearing your ring," Melissa pressed at his finger, as though making sure it was absent. "Out looking for trouble?" she asked, her breath felt hot on his neck.

"I found it," he replied, his hand tucked safely into the small of her back. "I'm knee deep in it, well passed treading water. I could swim, but I really don't mind sinking a little lower this evening."

"People will talk," she ran a finger up and down his ribs, under his jacket.

"Let them," he said, pausing on his heel. Devan span Melissa out. With a flick his wrist, he had her spinning back into his personal space. Back within a heartbeat and losing breath.

"You're playing with me," she narrowed her eyes, her grip on his fingers tightened. "I'm not a game, Devan; I'm not a toy."

"I know," he somewhat hissed his sharp response. His mood had become a little darker. "I just needed to make sure; stretch my boundaries. The boundaries that are back in place."

"You don't trust yourself," she tugged at his arm, knocked his leg with a heel as the riff twanged into a tango.

Devan tightened his own grip; he could feel the warmth of Melissa's skin radiate towards him with renewed intensity. He really couldn't stand the tango. It was the weirdest form of foreplay known to man.

"I don't trust *you*," he replied, jerking his head sharply. "I made my bed, doesn't mean you have to lie in it. Not again, not ever."

"You could have left me for the tow truck," her words were staccato across strings and brass.

"Shoulda, woulda, coulda," Growled Devan, dropping Melissa across his knee.

Suspenders.

He caught a flash of suspenders.

She had her hands full, she held onto his shirt and jacket.

This was too close. This was dangerous.

As the tango hummed away, Devan drew Melissa upright. The music changed as drums kicked in. All around them, couples started to samba.

"Take me home," whispered Melissa. She had unbuttoned his jacket, and now fiddled with his shirt. "Take me back, Devan; one last time."

He had closed his eyes; Melissa's fingers were splayed across his chest. His heart thumped that bit harder. It didn't know which way to send his blood. This had been all too simple. He had no faith in Melissa. The least he could, was have faith in himself.

Slowly, Devan pulled away, with her hands in his.

"We're done," he said letting her hands fall. He buttoned up his jacket, not looking her in the eye. "In every single aspect; I'll find another accountant."

With that, Devan turned his back to leave. As he left, he was called every name under the sun, loudly at that. The whole association stood, open-mouthed, watching a spectacle. Melissa ran after him too. As the car service left with him in the back, a spike heel hit the bumper.

Devan didn't look back. He simply couldn't.

She'd been right. He hadn't trusted himself. Not one bit. He certainly couldn't have trusted her.

They were done now. Completely and utterly, done.

Devan chose to lay low for a few days after. There would be ripples from the event. These ripples would eventually find him in the otherwise, quiet and stable

Peace. He was a hermit all right; holed up in the relative safety of Oakview.

There had been a few 'phone calls. A few concerned business associates, wanting to know what the drama had been. They all wanted to know, if there was anything that they ought to be aware of, lest their names be sullied. Each one had been softened, placated; Devan volunteered some of his Montana Moonshine to smooth ruffled feathers. Such were the trials of playing a character. The Hooch Baron wasn't going to be everyone's cup of tea. Staying indoors, Devan avoided Main Street. He didn't need to welcome any more would be ripples.

As he stood in the kitchen, Devan washed up at the sink. On the window sill, there was an upturned glass. A pale blue, hi-ball glass that gleamed in the sunlight; it was perfectly ordinary.

Underneath it, lay his wedding ring. It had been there, ever since he had come back from Billings. He'd brought it back in his pocket, put it there and not thought about it.

Devan eyed it as he placed dishes into the drying rack. Soap suds streaked the crockery.

What was he to do?

Devan Coultrie, was a tad lost.

□

# Chapter 12

Devan would surface from his solitude. The distinct lack of milk, eggs and a loaf forced him to go out to Brightman's. He was just about pick up a handbasket as his pocket vibrated. He was still avoidant of most people; Jericho and Jay had both been sent a vague text message. There was still no desire to engage with the world at large.

Sliding his 'phone from his pocket, he noticed the caller ID. Accepting the call, he made no greeting.

"Devan."

The way in which she rolled his name; it was as though she had run a finger salaciously down his spine. He automatically dropped the handbasket.

"It's Pudding. Devan, I need you. I can't do this by myself. I'm at Fur Family. Kayley let me bring her in. Please, Devan; I don't know what to do."

Hanging up, Devan tucked the device back into his pocket. A lesser man would've carried on shopping. Heading back the way he had come, Devan turned off Main Street onto Willow Brook lane. Fur Family was halfway down and easy to get to. He ambled, took his time. Devan needed to gather himself. Stepping into the clinic, Devan closed the door behind him. He nodded at Kayley behind the desk. She waved back whilst on the 'phone.

Kayley's eyes darted left, he mirrored the movement. He stood still as Aditi's heels squeaked across the floor. A screwed-up ball of tissue fell from her hands as she stood before him. Aditi's hair was scrapped back into a ponytail. Even without a scrap of make-up, she still glowed. She looked tired, angry and above all, she looked hurt.

"Poisoned," Aditi sobbed as she spoke. Tears tumbled down her face, a couple moved in parallel down lips. "Pudding has been poisoned. She's really unwell and might not make it."

Poisoned. Devan's heart sank, his mouth fell agape. He quickly snapped it shut.

He knew exactly who the culprit might be.

"If she gets worse," Aditi sniffed, licking away tears. "If she falls asleep, it'll break my heart. I can't lose her. She's my baby."

Suddenly, he couldn't feel his arms. Her pain, he could feel every last bit.

"Aditi. Devan."

Hearing his name, Devan span his head towards the door to the surgery. The vet was ashen-faced and removed latex gloves.

Aditi fell to her knees. Devan sprang forward to catch her. His wife vibrated with sheer agony as he took her into his arms.

An hour later, Devan all but carried Aditi home. He led her to the sofa, draped a blanket around her. There was no hesitation in raiding the liquor cabinet. He administered two fingers of brandy before Aditi fell into his arms. There was nothing he could say or do; all he could do was hold her. He really didn't want her to leave, especially not like this.

"Can I stay?" she asked, a little while later. It was almost as though she had read his mind. Dusk had fallen; time had ebbed away with grief.

Devan kissed the top of her head; his arms held her tighter, closer. There was no need to answer.

Aditi sobbed herself to sleep. Devan unfurled his arms to lay her across the sofa, encased in the blanket. He tucked her in, wanting to keep her safe. At that moment, he felt useless. He had no idea, where the lines were between them.

Leaving Aditi on the sofa, Devan made his way upstairs. He was tired, hungry too; only he didn't want to crash around in the kitchen. He took one last look at Aditi, before heading up and turning in. Perhaps things would look better in the morning.

Devan wasn't subdued by sleep for long. He was jostled awake as the covers were pulled back.

"What on earth?" he had no time to protest as Aditi clambered in alongside. She had invaded from his side, forcing him to shuffle over.

"You forgot this," she fumbled around, eventually grasping his left hand. "Left it on the sink," Aditi tugged at his fingers, to slide his wedding band back onto his finger.

He had forgotten, yes. Deliberately.

"And me," Aditi tugged at his green t-shirt. "Take me back too, Devan." Her legs had him hemmed in, unable to move.

"Pudding," Devan stumbled over the name. "You're only doing this because of Pudding. You're hurting, angry too. Don't make me a band-aid bunk up, Aditi." He regretted saying it immediately. "Is that what you want?" he really wasn't doing himself any favours.

Aditi nodded. He could make out that much in the dark.

"I want you," she whispered. "All of you."

That was all he needed to hear. Sleep could wait. Devan surrendered, to a woman heartbroken and awash with grief. There were worse things he could be, than a band-aid bunk up and at 2 a.m.

# Chapter 13

Aditi stayed. She cried off work and stayed for a week. During that week, Devan felt as though he was in a time-warp. Every moment, every minute was a reflection of what had been before Chris had called. This was a whole different universe.

Standing at the stove, Devan stirred scrambled eggs. His brows had knitted together in concentration; he checked, and double checked the heat. The eggs had been dosed with chives, tarragon and a dash of paprika.

"No one does eggs like you," Aditi declared, her arms snaked around his waist. Her hands clasped together over his stomach.

He could feel his wife breathe in and out. Then there was the way that she nudged toes up and down his calf. It was taking every bit of strength he had not turn around and cave in. At the moment, Aditi was jumping on him for every moment of afternoon delight she fancied.

A boy had to eat, and so did his wife.

"Make yourself useful," Devan spluttered as Aditi slid her hand below his t-shirt. "Stop with the tickling and make some tea. I need all the caffeine that I can get." He let out a wince as Aditi goosed his backside before peeling away.

"You could've said no," stated Aditi, filling a kettle. Tea would be made traditionally, with a saucepan.

"I did," Devan tutted as he cranked up the heat on the eggs. "Twice, before you pouted, lulled me and then took full advantage. I'm crying groin strain," he waggled a spatula at his wife. "You're on notice til teatime. I'm injured. In the meantime, sort yourself out."

Aditi pulled a face, poking out her tongue. "Spoil sport," she busied herself sorting out the bits and pieces she needed to make tea. There were tea bags, spice mix and a saucepan; the freshly drawn and boiled water to combine it all.

"You're leaving in the morning?" he asked, tentatively.

Aditi nodded as water was poured the pan. Tea bags were tossed in, spice mix too.

"I'll be back though," she replied, using a spoon to stir the tea as it brewed. "I won't need to stay in Billings as much, now that the office is up and running. Gives me more space and time with you."

"I'd like that," Devan half-smiled as he plated up eggs. A Full English was already made up and sat on the worktop. "Aditi…." He deliberately rolled the syllables of her name. There was a massive thought brewing in his head.

The two of them; man and wife stood toe to toe with one another.

"If I asked you to marry me," Devan had pulled his robe back: his hands were planted on his hips. He would've made a good breakfast superhero. "Even after everything, would you still marry me?"

"What again?" Aditi fiddled with her hear, coiling it up and away into a ponytail. "Yes, probably. It was fun the first time, albeit a bit chaotic. A renewal," she said wiggling a manicured finger. "That would make more sense." She turned away toward the 'fridge to grab a milk carton. "What is it, three years and counting?"

"Shall we?" he asked, both brows arched. "Not so much as tornado this time either. A proper family shin-dig; Libby and Rohan can bring Theo. Aida would want to be part of it. You could ask your brother. They all missed it the first time 'round. This would be making amends."

Aditi threw him a look at the mention of her brother. The two of them didn't exactly get on. Devan didn't particularly care for him either. This was, however, an attempt at reconciliation.

"Would I get to plan it?" Aditi crossed her arms as the tea bubbled. "I'd want full autonomy; we had a massive great big red wedding. We should probably make this a white one."

Nodding, Devan stepped down his superhero stance. "Well, yes," he said, tying his robe. "That makes sense. All I have to do is find a suit and turn up. I'll be there. I promise."

Letting rip with a squeal, Aditi bounded toward him with hers open wide. There were even dramatic, over-blown kisses that almost had Devan keeling over.

"We can do this," Aditi coiled a leg around his. "You and I, this is worth fighting for, Devan. Nothing else matters."

The scrambled eggs, and the rest, would go cold. Devan's groin strain, as fake as it was, would become very real. Aditi left the next morning, having lobbed a bag of frozen peas at him.

There was planning to do. Six weeks later, there would be a renewal. A renewal of something worth fighting for.

He held Aditi to that. Every inch of her.

"So this is everything?" Devan asked, taking a slurp of ice-cold lemonade. He'd spent an hour on the 'phone, yelling at an incompetent fund-raiser who worked for a state charity. He needed the drink; his throat was red raw.

"Everything," Aditi nodded, flicking through a folder of preparations. "The itinerary, order of service, and a couple of menus."

Devan followed along as the pages turned. "Wait, hold up," he said, landing a palm across two pages. "I don't remember that," he tapped a finger across canapes and cocktails.

"That's for the reception," replied Aditi, her eyelashes fanned and fluttered.

"No," his tone was terse as his stomach lurched. "Fizz and fruit juice will do. There's a whole five course dinner too," Devan glared at his wife. "And you've butchered my vows," he flicked a page, to run his finger down a page full of scribble. "Please don't put words into mouth. Plus, it was all good the first time." He bit the inside of his cheek; his hackles had risen to well beyond half-mast.

"Devan," Aditi uttered his name so softly, it was barely audible. Her hand moved to his, her fingers cupped around his. "What's the matter, you've been sore for days. If this is all too much. We can the whole thing.

*'We can the whole thing'.*

The phrase hit a nerve and pulled it taut.

The thought had crossed Devan's mind: a few times at that, whilst doing cartwheels. It wasn't a pleasant thought.

"God, no," his eyes snapped wide. "No way," he added, shaking his head whilst wiggling his hand free. Aditi's fingers were heavier than he remembered. "I'm sorry," Devan let out a short breath, passing his palms across his face. "I had a fight with a numpty earlier. It's not you, not this; it's me. I need to go take a walk."

Devan looked at Aditi through his fingers. She looked all too exasperated, all too clueless of what was going on inside his head. He'd barely spoken to her over the last few days, to dodge all of the planning that she'd been doing.

"I'm sore, as I work with idiots," he pronounced. That was a lie, a complete and utter whopper. "This is not about the renewal," he said, rising from the table. Slinging back lemonade, Devan drained the can.

Aditi pouted at him, as she scooped up the renewal paraphernalia. He watched her eyes narrow. That was her 'cut the crap' look; a look that he really didn't care for. He wondered how much of her, he did care for. Everything was a mess.

"Go take walk," she said finally. There was even genteel nod as she stacked her paperwork. "I love you. Okay?"

"I know," he half smiled, it felt like a reflex. "I love you too." He couldn't help but say it back. Despite what had happened, it was hard not to respond. "You want me gone though," he bit his lip to tuck in his chair. "You bought a steak dinner, and don't want me to hover."

His wife pointed to the door out of the walled garden. "Go," she said, smirking a little. "Come back in an hour. Medium rare?" she asked, tilting her head.

"As you wish," he said, picking up a notepad and his pens. "Just don't burn anything," he said, not even looking over his shoulder as he left.

"Yeah, yeah, flames of passion," trilled Aditi. "Not real ones."

Devan rolled his eyes as exit. He couldn't trust Aditi with their marriage, trusting her with his kitchen was just as risky.

Leaving the house, he headed toward an outbuilding. There were over half a dozen dotted around the 100-acre estate. Each one was a dilapidated shell of a structure, which like Devan, required TLC. This particular building was two storey's high and freshly re-modelled. He entered and stood in the middle of what could be a lounge. The whole building was a mirror-image of what he and his wife now called 'The Main House'.

Wrinkling up his nose, Devan grimaced at the freshly plastered, salmon-coloured walls. Eventually, he would get around to making it all look pretty. He was thinking about renting it out, making something of a profit. The other buildings would meet a similar fate. He had half a mind to turn them over to community use. It would give him something other than his wife to worry about.

Retreating to Peace, had taken on different slant. Here he was, about to renew vows that had been badly betrayed, broken and cast aside.

His notebook and pen cascaded from his arms to land with a thud upon concrete.

"What have I done?" he asked out aloud, his words bounced off the walls. "I could've been a better man. She chose me. Aditi chose me."

His words had become a roar, hit the walls to the box his ears.

"It could've all been so perfect," he lowered his tone, to mutter to himself. "Betrayal works both ways. She's no better; I'm no worse. No rhyme, no reason. No God-damned excuse."

Feeling acid reflux travel up his gullet, Devan pulled a face. Placing a palm to his breast-bone, he felt wretched all over. He made a mental note to stay off the bourbon a while. Betrayal had one hell of a left-hook. Devan hadn't felt the same since he taken that 'phone call.

Then there was the illicit dalliance he was partaking in.

He had no idea which would cave first. His body or his conscience.

Devan felt like crap. Absolute crap.

For two minutes he listened to the blood rush around his ears.

"I'm not a crap hole," he told himself. "I never was. I wouldn't know how. All I did, was dare to dream; dream of jam-making in Montana. This wasn't about being in hell but chasing a piece of heaven. You almost had it. Funny thing, Coultrie, you still could."

He could, if he didn't talk himself out of it. What he needed was help.  He needed someone else to stop him from being stupid. Feeling clamminess beneath his fingers, Devan held onto his 'phone. Wiping the device across his thighs, he unlocked it to make a call.

He took a punt; he never remembered the time difference. Right now, he really didn't care. Devan Coultrie would have his counsel regardless. Tapping call, he held the device to his ear. The dial tone synced in time to his racing heart.

"Am I being an idiot?" he asked; it was an unusual greeting. "This vow renewal: a fresh start or sheer stupidity."

For thirteen seconds, there was nothing but dead air. What broke it was the Anglo-Saxon directive for going forth and procreating.

"Do you know what time it is, Devan?" The voice was altogether screechy. "It's your brother. He's having a moment. Hold on. You're going on loudspeaker. Just don't shout. The baby has only just gone to sleep. Go."

Devan winced as Libby issued her imperative. He'd forgotten the time difference and the baby.

"Do I go through with this vow renewal?" he asked, once more.

"Yes, you bloody well do," replied Rohan. It had been him, who had sworn. "We've paid to come, bought new clothes. Else I will unleash a sleep deprived child at you. Kid's also teething. How'd you feel about dodgy poop….." His voice trailed off a little.

"This was your idea, Devan," Libby butted in sharply. "You suggested it after the cat died. You were all doe-eyed and delirious. We couldn't get a word in edgewise. For the love of God, Coultrie, she did the dirty on you."

Devan heard Rohan try to shush her.

"I tried, Rohan tried," continued Libby. "Does Aida know yet?"

Feeling his face flush, Devan cleared his throat a couple of times. "No," he replied, sheepishly. "Don't think I want her to know."

"Mum, Dad?" Rohan chimed in. "That would be like summoning the four horsemen of the apocalypse."

Shaking his head, Devan rolled his eyes. He may have been stupid a few times over. But he was yet to be certified.

"No," he replied, coughing a little. "And you're both sworn to secrecy on the pain of moonshine."

"I can drink that now!" exclaimed Libby. "Idle threat there, dear boy. I know where you stash it all."

"Don't tempt her," Rohan tutted across the line. "Look, only you can do this. Only you can decide. Not as though you've done the same and played away."

Devan groaned; bile was starting to rise again.

"Wait, hold on," Rohan sighed, there was the sound of muttering. "Libby wants to talk to you. Plus, the baby is awake. I'll check with sproglet."

"Devan?" Libby said his name as the bedroom door creaked. "It's me, not loudspeaker. "

Pressing the 'phone closer to his ear, Devan shuffled on the spot. His feet nudged at the pen and pad that were dropped earlier.

"Lib, you didn't tell him?" he posed, all too furtively.

"I couldn't," whispered Libby. "You told me, because you were breaking apart. That," she said, her tone softened. "Was brave, but even I'm not stupid. You trusted me."

"He'd go bat crap crazy," stated Devan. "He'd be pissed with Aditi."

"Yes, he'd nail you to the bloody wall," commented Libby, spitting out the words. "Don't do it, Coultrie. For your own sake, you deserve so much more."

"And look, Mummy's awake too!" Rohan crowed across the line. "Time for cuddles; but what about your stinky bottom?"

"I'd best see to it," replied Libby. "Gotta go, Dev. See you in Peace." With that, his esteemed sister-in-law hung up.

Now he was torn further, none the wiser. The renewal had been his idea, to mend things. He had expected nothing less than frankness from Libby. Bending, Devan picked up his pen and pad. He'd skulk around, kill some more time. Devan Coultrie, was in something of a mess.

□

# Chapter 14

The renewal; it soon came around. After all the planning, Devan and Aditi eventually got the show on the road. His siblings arrived, parents too. Aditi's parents made the journey across, dragging her brother along.

"You're all very smiley, yes, you are," Devan was getting to know his nephew a little better as they all waited for Aditi to arrive. A twenty five by fifty foot tent had been erected in the middle of Oakview for the ceremony. He and Theo giggled with kisses and cuddles. "And back to Mummy we go."

Libby arched a brow to take Theo back. She pressed a slice of cucumber into the boy's hand. "You agreed to all of this," she told him, eying the entrance as Rohan stepped in. He like Devan was dressed in a Midnight Blue suit and tie. In his button hole, was a pale pink Peace Rose.

"I know," nodded Devan, rubbing his palms together. "And look," he pointed at Theo. The boy was taking great delight in wiping his hands across his mother's pale blue, silk dress.

"Oh, Theo," tutted Libby, smiling as she kissed her son's hands. "Batter, up," she said stepping aside as Rohan walked down the aisle.

Taking the hint, Devan moved towards a canopy covered in all the Peace roses that Aditi had got her hands on. Rohan arrived to stand next to him.

"I've wished her luck," he said quietly. "Better luck, for this time," he added. "That's the last thing that I ever want to say to her. You might forgive and forget, but I don't have to."

Devan shushed his brother, shoved him aside so that they could both see the entrance. Twenty seconds passed, the harpist twanged her strings to play 'Stand By Me.'

Accompanied by her father and her brother, Aditi made her way down the aisle. She wore her hair loose, in ringlets. She was a vision in white duchess satin embellished with lace, pearls and crystals.

Meeting him at the canopy, Devan held out both his hands.

Aida finally broke the silence as she stood before them. She had missed out on being bridesmaid, so had been asked to be the celebrant. Her hands trembled as she clutched onto a sheet of pale pink paper.

Devan tipped her a wink; he loved his little sister dearly. Her hands immediately stopped shaking.

"So," began Aida, smiling softly. "Here we are. Devan, wanted to get married again. Aditi, agreed. Same vows," she giggled, waving the paper. "Not so chaotic this time though. Let's do this, once more with lots of feeling. Devan, repeat after me…."

He did, as did Aditi. There was renewal. There was also a honeymoon this time.

Two days later, as the family departed, Aditi and Devan also boarded a plane. They flew via London, with Devan keeping his wife in the dark about the destination.

"Geneva?" she had asked, boarding their connection.

"Blame the Bollywood movies," he had replied. "Looks epic. If they liked it, why won't we?" he had shrugged but grinned too.

They had mooned around the lake; in a similar vein to when Aditi had first arrived in Peace. Devan let himself go, he let Aditi take his breath away. Then there was Chamonix, where he really did lose his breath.

"Mont Blanc?" Aditi had gasped at the sight through her sunglasses. They had scaled the peak next to it in a cable-car.

The whole trip was spent rekindling and renewing. There would be consequences.

Those, would be dealt with, in Montana. □

# Chapter 15

Yellow Lentils; they were the answer to everything. When you though the world was ending, and couldn't stomach anything, yellow lentils worked. Stirring them in a saucepan, Devan put the lid on half way. This was the second batch this week; he was bored of eating them. Only this wasn't about him; not really. For the last week, Aditi had roamed around Oakview, all very green behind the gills. She had cancelled her whole life, including work to stay at home. Naturally, Devan was worried; the words 'in sickness and health' were freshly inked across his mind.

"Do you want some mint tea, Aditi, ginger, perhaps?" he asked. She was sat nearby, her head resting on her arms.

Looking up, Aditi gulped. She had gone an interesting shade of green. He chair moved backward, she headed for the sink.

"Tomorrow, we go to the doctor," he told her, reaching for a towel. "Hang the bloody insurance. You're not right. Yellow lentils, Aditi, aren't going to cover this."

Dutifully, Devan took his wife to the doctors. Only for her to be admitted to St. Vincent's, pretty damned quickly.

"Mrs.Coultrie, you're not sick. You're pregnant. This is morning sickness in the worst degree. We'll need to keep you in for a while. You really can't go on like this."

Sat on the edge of Aditi's bed, Devan watched the doctor leave. Turning to his wife, Devan saw a wide-eyed, scared looking expression.

"You said," he bit his lip, trying not to laugh. "That you couldn't fit into anything. After we came back from Geneva, none of your work clothes looked right. You told me off, for making you square meals. Then there was the whole couple's diet thing, in solidarity."

"You're not funny," she said, pouting at him. "Half of this is your fault entirely."

"Oh, and another thing," the doctor was back, peeking behind a door. "We should arrange a sonogram."

"We haven't got two up there, have we?" Devan's eyes narrowed, somewhat in jest. "I mean, really?"

The doctor suggested that they check. Extreme morning sickness was one thing, but twins were another hypothesis worth exploring.

A hypothesis confirmed by the sonogram. Devan's square meals really weren't at fault.

With Aditi rigged up to a drip, he remained at her side. The medics wanted to keep an eye on her. She was too poorly for their liking; not to mention, a little further on that originally thought.

"This is all very scary," she had said, wiping a palm across her nose. They had both been in tears during the scan. She clutched at a still that had been taken. "Two, very grainy, but strangely beautiful, splodges."

"Just a bit," nodded Devan. He too was mesmerised by the image. He'd very nearly fallen off his chair when two heartbeats had been played. They had declined knowing about gender.

"We don't do things by halves," he commented, placing a hand to Aditi's knees. "It's scary, but a good scary."

Aditi was kept in for a few more days. Devan loitered, watching everything. Suddenly, his life had become a little more complex. Sharing it with Aditi was one thing, but now they were having babies.

He asked that she stay at Oakview, worked remotely; it would make things easier. Aditi agreed, but the apartment in Billings would stay. Just in case. They had come to an agreement. This wasn't just about having babies, this was about having a whole world.

The world wasn't done changing. It would throw one more curved ball.

Aditi had been home for less than three days. A makeshift office was created in the second bedroom. The third would be the nursery. Devan had come upstairs; he was about to cook dinner. What he wanted to do know, was did his wife want peas or Climbing French Beans.

The door was ajar; his wife was deep in conversation.

"We ended the day you killed Pudding," yelled Aditi. "I know why you did it-I know it was you-you know why. You always were a crap-hole, Chris. Yep, I got sucked in; I destroyed a perfectly good-"

Devan pushed the door open. He loomed large over the threshold.

Aditi Rao looked at him dead on. Her phone was pressed to her ear.

"I destroyed a perfectly good marriage," she kept talking, her gaze didn't waver. "I broke every single vow. So when Devan broke your nose, knocked the crap out of you in that alley…."

Devan closed his eyes as his blood ran cold.

"He's not perfect either," Aditi gulped, before clearing her throat. "Talks in his sleep."

His eyes snapped open. Aditi glared back. She looked into the darkest depths of his soul.

"I cheated on him, with you," she continued, licking away a tear. "He had his accountant. As for you, Chris. Never again."

Hanging up, Aditi threw her 'phone across the room.

This was no longer a shattered peace.

This was Peace Betrayed.

# Epilogue

Two sets of hands. Two pairs of feet. Four lungs that were healthy and noisy. That was just a small aspect of the two children that arrived at the end of a hot, heavy and rather chaotic weekend. Aditi laboured over three days; the children really weren't in a rush.

There had been no time to get to St.Vincents. Instead, the master bedroom had become a hub of activity. A homebirth had only ever been a vague plan. In becoming a reality, it had thrown everyone for a loop. There was however medical care, everyone was safe. The babies were a low-risk delivery, thankfully.

Suraj had arrived first. Devan had almost caught him as Aditi had paced. The boy had screamed like there was no tomorrow. His face all pink and screwed up.

Aditi had elbowed Devan out the way. "Cord," she had yelled. "You should cut the cord."

He had done as he was told. Minutes later, there were kisses and cuddles all around.

Suraj Aaron Coultrie weighed in at six pounds and eight.

It was twenty minutes before the next round. Suraj was handed over to a grandparent as Devan and Aditi paced once more. Devan recoiled as Aditi threw a punch at him. He had ducked when he heard the cry pierce the air.

Sagar Richard Coultrie also arrived kicking and screaming. A little bigger than his brother, he weighed just over six pounds ten.

Later, as Aditi braved a bath, Devan stood over the two bassinets in the nursery. He had so many stories to tell his two boys.

Fiddling with Sagar's toes, Devan rubbed Suraj's belly. He knew something, felt something bigger than he could ever comprehend.

He felt love, and a whole lot of Peace.

Finally.

## About the Author

Punam Farmah is a teacher, a counsellor and lives in Birmingham, England. She is very appreciative of the help from the rest of her family and acknowledges that without them, this book would be devoid of any words, motivation or happy thoughts. When not teaching or counselling, she rather likes Star Trek, Shakespeare and the Whedon-verse.

To follow along with all of her adventures:
www.horticulturalhobbit.com
www.twitter.com/horticulturalh
Also on Facebook, Search for Petal: Horticultural 'Obbit

Other works:
Playing with Plant Pots: Tales from the allotment
Sow, Grow and Eat: From plot to kitchen
Fragments
Kangana
Retreating to Peace: A Peace Series Novella
Postcards from Peace: A Peace Series Collection

## Acknowledgments

Once more, I would like to thank S. H. Pratt for allowing me to make another contribution to the Peace Novella Series. This felt like the right thing to do with Devan and his Peace Journey. It has been one of the most wonderful writing adventures, and I'm really glad to have been part of this project. Peace is something that will always be a big part of me.

As such, I give a nod to all the other authors in the Peace stable for their unwavering support and encouragement.

Last but not least, to my family and friends who have listened to me witter on about Devan Coultrie over the last three years. He's been an interesting figment of my imagination, and they've all known about it.

Peace Continues
You can find more details about Peace at:
Facebook.com/PeaceSeriesNovella

Other Peace Titles:
Songs of Peace by A. H. Stagg
Love in Peace by Krysi Foster
What Peace Remains by L.C Fenton
Reclaiming Peace by S.H Pratt
Seeking Peace by S. H. Pratt
A Haven in Peace by Cassie May
Peace and Comfort by Jeanetta Sneed
Peace and Harmony by Lisa Ann
The Philosophy of Peace by Jennifer Fisch-Ferguson
A Dusty Road to Peace by Tee Smith
Peace in the Storm by S. Jackson Rivera
Accepting Peace by Jenn Braddock
Peace of Work by Rachel Walter
Peace Out by Sandra Hurst
Peace in Flames by Caroline Andrus
Summer of Peace by Caroline Andrus
Beautiful Master Peace by Gabriela Lizette

Retreating to Peace

A Peace Series novella by Punam Farmah

Devan Coultrie was at a loss. His world had been shaken, his heart fractured and emptied by death. In search of a way to heal and shake of the damage, Devan sticks a pin a map with the intention of going wherever it lands. Leaving the shores of the United Kingdom, he ends up Stateside, deep in the heart of Montana. With all of his worldly possessions, Devan drives into Peace and onto a plot to land to start life over.

Like him, the farm and its acreage is downbeat, derelict and defeated. When Aditi Rao arrives in Peace, Devan's plans for himself and his home are disrupted. He has history with Aditi and she'd quite like to write another chapter. Can he show Aditi that his retreat to Peace is more than just a plot of land and on a different continent? Can he find a way to share his home, his heart and a new beginning?

Postcards from Peace

A Peace Series novella by Punam Farmah

In Retreating to Peace, Devan Coultrie moved kit and caboodle to Montana. Before long, he was joined by Aditi Rao. Their history laid the foundations for a rosy future together. Devan now calls Peace home and his life has become eventful.

This collection of short stories sees his family visit, his romance with Aditi develop further and his dreams in Peace blossom.

Devan Coultrie's life in Peace is a picture postcard with more to it than meets the eye.

Made in the USA
Monee, IL
21 October 2026

66035050R00078